1.

COOT

Written by Jennifer Jupie Thompson...

Copyright 2009, A One Finger Production...

Long ago when the world was young; a son was born to proud parents that had waited a very long time for a child.

Now that their long waited child is born.

A great feast was prepared.

People of the mighty kingdom joined in the celebration also, because they too were happy for their King and Queen.

The child was like no other child ever born in the land.

He was perfect in every way.

People of the land had never seen such a perfect child, and that made the parents very proud.

As their Son grew.

The people of the land often notice his love of bow and arrows.

They made him several kinds.

The little girls of the land often flocked around him.

None of the other little boys were notice by the little girls as much.

The little girls even loved the sound of his name.

But not him.

A name he did not care for at all.

His parents named him Swoot, but he preferred to be called Coot.

Matter of fact, it was the only name he would answer to.

Being called Coot did not matter to his parents at all, because they loved him just that much.

Coot grew into a very handsome and strong young man.

Even he thought so.

He loved to hunt and had developed a passion for it.

His skill was unsurpassed.

Nothing he hunted could escape him.

Yes.

Hunting and women were at his disposal, being so carefree and young, enjoying all the attention he was getting from the young women.

Even though he had it all.

Other young men still enjoyed being with him, because they also enjoyed, some of the attention from some of the young women too.

Coot enjoyed hunting and killing of deer's, more than he cared for being with the young women.

They came second in his life.

This gave the other young men a chance to be noticed by some of the young women too.

One woman vowed she's going to capture Coot for her own; her father was to help her with the plan.

Because he despised Coot with A passion.

He called on all sorts of evil powers to help him.

But it will take time and he has to be very cautious; because Coots Father and

Mother had control of the people in the land they ruled.

No one in the land was about to let no harm come to their King and Queen precious Coot (no way).

The King wants Coot to belong his daughter badly; it was all he thought about night and day, day after day.

Primarily how to capture Coot for his daughter

Coot saw her as he did the other young women that wanted most of his time.

Something he was not giving any of them.

The woman that wants' him for her own her name is Molive.

A very beautiful woman.

But evil same as her Father.

Who wanted a son instead.

So he instilled evil in his daughter.

Something his Queen did not approve of at all.

Especially their plans on destroying Coot.

She adored Coot and loved to see him riding his stallion in town showing off the many deer's him and the others had slayed.

In the lands, deer meat were of great importance; but everyone couldn't get the meat.

It took a very skilled and successful hunter to get the meat that was gravely wanted through-out the lands.

Coot so much like his father.

Whose also is a skillful hunter he too helped at times bring riches to the land. Coot did agree with his Father hunting if he was a servant; he asked his Father never again come with his band of hunters and him; he is to remain in his Castle and rule the people of his land.

As King.

People of other lands paid large sums of money, to have just a little piece of deer meat; the more they wanted it; the more some paid for it.

People from all other land's looked to Coot's Father more than any other Kingdom.

Now Coot.

is the one they look to even more; and that made his Father proud.

Coot and other hunters went from forests to forests hunting and slaying deer's; it was no one among him that he trusted, none of his hunters was to know how he slayed a deer.

All they saw when he went to the slayed animal. Coot and his hunters brought back other slayed animals too, but of course deer meat was the most important prize.

Coot made certain they only brought the largest of deer's weighing over 200lbs; not only would they have 10; at times 30 or more.

People of the lands would be standing in lines on end, sometime days; waiting to buy the precious meat.

Molive's Father refuse to stand in line; instead he would send several of his servants from his Kingdom.

His plan was to get them close to Coot; to find out how he slayed deer's, then his Kingdom would be richer also. But that was to never happen.

Coot's own Father had no clue how his Son hunted or what method he used. The people of Molive Father's land ate the meat of fowl, rabbits, chicken, and pork.

When they taste the well season deer meat; they preferred it over the other meat even more.

That made them cling to Coot Father's Kingdom even more too; they was willing and paid for the meat at higher prices than the others.

Molive's Father were getting more evil each passing day; the mentioning of Coot's name made him angry.

All kind of evil thoughts were building up in his mind, horrible ways in destroying Coot; he was thinking with Coot gone, the people of the lands would come to him for the precious meat.

But why would they?

He had no hunters with the knowledge of hunting deer.

Molive's Father held a meeting with several of his trusted allies; he commanded them to search far and wide; in finding ways to destroy Coot once and for all.

His Daughter will have to find another suitor to fall in love with.

Unknowing to him Molive heard the whole conversation.

She approached her Father.

To his amazement she was not angry with him at all.

She told her Father he has her full support in destroying Coot.

She no longer wants him for her own anymore.

If she couldn't have him.

No woman will.

Sone of Molive father's trusted friends told him about an old woman; that lives at the edge of the black forest.

That has power that comes from deep within it forest; so deep most men dare to venture there.

And that will be their way in destroying Coot.

His trusted friend also told him.

My King there is a terrible price to pay if you visit this old woman.

The King angrily asked.

WHAT KIND OF PRICE?

The man told him the price is, who-ever go to her might not ever return.

The King yelled.

Even if it's twenty men?

How can an old woman defeat twenty men?

Is this old witch alone?

Yes the man said; why does she need anyone when she has the power to protect herself?

The King told his trusted men; I have to think harder about this one.

One day Coot was sitting and talking with his Father.

The King wanted his son to start thinking about his future.

He said Son, you are a man and you should be thinking about being a husband and father.

Coot laughed out loud.

I am not ready to be with one woman for the rest of my life; when there are thousands at my beck and call.

Sorry Father, I am not ready to hang up my bow and arrows yet.

I'm having too much fun letting some of the women of the land chase after me.

Father no other man throughout the lands are greater than me, Coot boasted.

The King was very displeased with his son's bragging remarks.

He told his son to never think other men are beneath him when it came to women.

The only difference between you and other men, is you are A Prince.

But it still don't give you the right to brag or belittle other men of this land; you will give some reasons to harm you even kill.

NEVER boast to me again in that manner.

NEVER!

The King turned and walked away.

He went to his royal chambers and had a talk with his Queen; about the conversation he had with their Son.

The Queen said, when you entered our room the look on your handsome face, let me know something is serious wrong; so tell me everything that's bothering you concerning our Son.

Swoot is becoming something that's going to bring harm to him the King sadly said.

Yes our Son is a very skillful hunter; and majority of the women of the land is at his feet, but he cares nothing for any of them at all, not even the other Kings daughters

Some of the men of this land despise him; because he take their women only because he can.

Afterwards he has nothing to do with them. Just move on to the next one waiting to be in his clutch.

Swoot must change his ways soon.

I know he's made our Kingdom the riches throughout all the lands; but that won't stop some from wanting to destroy or even kill him.

Coot's Mother didn't want to hear about how others would want to kill her precious Son. She was thinking of having a talk with him also.

The Queen had to admit, she loves the attention her son is receiving; he and other hunters did provide the precious deer meat that the people of lands craved for. So if some of the women flocked at his feet.

So What!

He's my handsome Son.

It could be in another manner.

Him putting out messages for the attention of women.

The Queen sat quietly and let her King continue talking about their Prince; but there was no way in her mind she wanted things differently. Coot is of great importance and the people of the lands should bow and praise him.

He earned all the glory he's receiving.

The King finish talking with his Queen. She prayed a prayer to God of protection; asking him to for-ever protect her Son from harm;

Others were also praying too

Not for the protection of Coot.

Only for capture.

Molive asked her Father to summon some of the men in their land to attend a very important meeting.

After all were gathered together Molive told them.

All of you is needed to go on a journey with me, to the edge of a forest to pay an old woman an overdue visit.

The men were showing signs of fear on their faces; one spoke and said, Princess we have heard about that forest and the old woman that lives close to it.

It's said she have strange powerful powers; and no man for over A thousand years dare to venture there.

Molive stood and pointed her finger at the man and asked him, how did you find out about this old woman and the forest?

Where you got your information from?

The man bowed his head and sadly said; Princess I'm only repeating what I heard from others that live in other lands.

Molive ordered the men; all of you is to come with me.

She assured them nothing is going to happen to any of them; all she wants is information from the old woman and telling them what kind of evil power dwells in the forest.

Molive's Father was shocked to hear his daughter talk in such a manner; she no longer had the look of beauty or innocence about her.

Just Evil.

Her father was feeling a great sense of guilt; knowing it is his fault; he's built a great amount of evil in his once beautiful daughter; and he knows there is no way out of it.

The damage is done.

Molive and some of the men from her father's Kingdom left to pay the old woman a visit; they brought valuable gifts of gold and the most valuable gift of all, a leg of deer meat.

Her mother was very angry with the King, for planting evil in their Daughters heart. Other Prince's wanted her too.

But the feelings she had for Coot, left no room in her heart for none others.

The Queen made a vow; she's going to win her daughter back.

That's when she decided to follow them to the old woman that lives close to this unknown forest.

Another celebration was being held, in honor of Coot and his hunters for another successful hunt.

Other food was brought from their hunt too; fruits no one had ever seen; the word about this strange fruit spread far and wide; each household of the land had this strange fruit (oranges) most importantly of all was the deer meat.

The deer meat was cleaned and prepared and the feast was on.

Some of the people that lived in other lands were invited; also their Kings and Queens.

Molive's Father told people of his land no one is to attend the feast at Coot Father's Kingdom; if he gets wind someone from his land attended they will be punish.

The people of his land knew too well how he punish someone if his rules are broken.

Pure Torture even Death.

His people wanted so badly to attend the festival at Coot Fathers Kingdom; so they could buy some of the deer meat;

The Queen was pleading with him to change his ruling.

It was to no avail.

His answer remained NO.

The Queen's mind continue thinking about following her daughter and the others to visit the old woman; and try to talk some sense into her, to end the crusade in trying to destroy Coot.

Meanwhile back at the Kingdom of Coot's father; several women were trying to get Coots attention.

He notice one woman in particular.

She was holding up a very beautiful well-crafted bow and arrow case.

Coot waved his hand to the crowd and they became quiet; he asked the woman to come forward.

The people were shocked to see this woman; because none of them knew where she come from.

The bow and arrow case that was placed before Coot; no one had ever seen a design as it before.

What land are you from?

Coot asked the beautiful woman; she responded.

I am from the land on the other side of the dark forest.

My hunters and I have hunted in many forests; we never heard of this dark forest before Coot responded.

Coot asked the woman about the crafted bow and arrow case; she responded to him by saying.

The people of my land has heard about you great hunter of deer's; and our crafted men made this gift for you.

Hoping you will reward our land with the precious meat majority of the lands enjoy.

Please accept this gift.

Coot was amaze how heavy the case is, to say it was being handed to him by a woman.

The woman asked him to test it out.

Coot took one of the arrows and placed it upon the bow and let the arrow flow; it sailed very smoothly hitting a tree.

Everyone at the feast was in awe.

When the arrow return back to Coot; still in midair in front of him, he took hold of the arrow and placed it back in the sheath with the others.

He looked to ask the woman about the gift.

She was nowhere in sight.

None of the others saw her leave.

The people were asking Coot to destroy the gift for black magic is on it.

Coot's heart was taken in by his gift.

Thinking how his hunting would be better than before.

His father was looking and thinking about his son saying within.

Now my son has magic bow and arrows that only obey him; we only know the gift come from some dark forest.

One he's never hunted in before.

Now to find this forest.

But How?

Coot never let his bow and arrows out of his sight; he didn't have to worry about them as he thought, because the arrows only obeyed him.

On his next hunt they brought more than ever before.

His father's kingdom was now more rich and powerful than ever.

But it also brought sadness to his Father's heart, he no longer wanted his son to hunt.

They have more riches than they will ever need.

But it was no stopping of Coot and his band of hunters.

His mother was enjoying the notoriety also other Mothers of the land.

Some of the men of the land were not enjoying any of it; because they did not want one man providing for their family.

Especially their women.

They hated their women thinking only how great Coot ass is.

Dam him being A Prince!

Majority of some were thinking; and it applied the same concerning his band of hunters too. They continue to envy Coot; more than his hunters.

Plotting in ways how to do it.

Something needs to be done.

BUT HOW?

Some men of the land met secretly to plot against Coot; they had to be very careful, because if anyone found out about their plotting.

The person behind it would surly die.

Coot went about his days doing what he's always done; having successful hunts and being catered to by majority of the women of the land, including his trusted hunters too.

WHAT A LIFE.

Coot was enjoying himself and didn't care how some of the other men felt at all; him and his band of hunters; had their pick of the litter of beautiful women and nothing was said or done about it.

In Molive's land it was the opposite.

They were being talked about in another manner especially by their King.

After traveling for days.

Molive finally made it to the old woman that lives close to the forest; after telling the old woman the reason they were there, it surprise them all when they were told.

She too has heard about this hunter name Coot.

Unknowing to Molive and the others her Mother was with them too, standing outside the old woman's front door.

The old woman's house looked of a raggedy shanty totally un-livable for a human being, especially to someone known of having great powers.

The old woman lit another candle.

That's when they all saw what she really looked like.

A horrible looking beast!

Something one only see in their worst nightmares; the old woman was telling them she's heard of Coot long before they paid her a visit.

She told them she sent one of her own to present him with a magical gift.

That only obeys him.

Molive asked her to tell them of this gift; her question was ignored.

Another asked the old woman.

Why Coot?

The old woman only smiled and said, I know a gift as that is what a great hunter like Coot would love to have for his own.

Molive told the old woman in an angry voice.

I CAME HERE TO FIND WAYS IN DESTROYING COOT!

The old woman said to Molive.

The only way to destroy a person as great as Coot; one must seek and find the thing that lives in this great forest that's behind me.

Why Coot and his band of hunters know nothing about this forest Molive asked?

The old woman asked them to step back outside.

Her Mother moved to the side still watching everything.

The old woman pointed to the sky and said, look around you; they saw nothing and asked her.

What happen to the woods?

They looked back at her and she was no longer an old woman.

BUT A BEAST.

Lumpy and fat with a head that had ten eyes.

They stood in fear as it spoke

I am the evil that lives deep in my forest and I am the one to capture this Coot. I been waiting a very long time for someone to visit me.

Not any of you will go back to tell that you been here.

Molive's Mother tried very hard to remain quiet; but the beast caught smelled of her and said, come out human woman or I will slay you where you stand.

Molive and the others were very surprise to see her.

Mother does father know you are here? Did you tell anyone in the Kingdom; about your decision to follow us here?

Father must be worried to death.

I know he know you are missing from the Castle. At this very moment he's gathering other men from our land and they are headed this way in search of you.

Molive! her mother replied.

I follow you all here to try and reason with you. Please give up this evil plot in destroying Coot. There are other suitors you can choose to be your own.

It's not love for Coot from you anymore; I see evil you are carrying in your heart for him now.

Your father is the blame for it!

So you are here now to try and change my mind?

Why Mother?

The beast refused to let her speak.

The men with Molive ask the beast, what do you want from us?

Slaves the beast answered.

I need slaves to dig in my woods forest floor.

The diamonds and gold nuggets that are buried in my forest dirt

Are you male or female Molive asked the beast.

NEITHER!

I am the evil that lives in weak human men.

What about my Mother and me Molive asked?

No one will ever know any of you came here the beast replied.

Molive told the beast, that's where you are wrong you ugly creature from Hell.

My father and others of our land know we venture here in search of you; and he and others will come looking for us.

No they will not the beast assured them.

There is no path to lead them here.

Molive's Mother yelled you ugly beast.

I WILL NEVER BELONG TO YOU OR MY DAUGHTER.

The beast said yes I know.

A human woman is never welcome in my forest; so today say your good byes to the Sun, with a blink of one of its slimy eyes,

Molive and her Mother were two beetle bugs crawling in circles on the dirt. The beast looked at the very frighten me that travel with Molive.

It knew they was under his command!

The beast ordered one of the men to crush the two beetle bugs with his boot.

It was done.

The beast said to the others, you all can work for me or return to the dirt from which you came; or you can live forever in my forest.

The men being frighten and thinking none of them wanted to die that day; they all bowed on bended knees and said to the beast.

We now serve you mighty one.

The beast smiled and told them.

Sure you all do.

All of you are slaves of my forest.

I am Master Wog.

That's what I am to be called by useless humans as you.

Wog told them, since you all is on bended knees you shall remain that way. Wog then turned the men into creatures of half man and toad.

They were a horrible sight.

And the first thing one of them did was; slurped up the two dead beetle bugs that was crushed on the dirt.

Wog blinked another one of its slimy eyes and the forest was restored; a very large beetle bug came up to him and asked.

What now Master?

It's time for you to go back to the darkness before your powers weaken. Wog said yes I shall, before others come looking for their worthless women.

What a Waste.

Who needs their worthless asses anyway?

The large beetle bug asked?

Master Wog.

What about the other woman that presented the magic gift to Coot?

She was only a figure of their imagination Wog answered, none of his Father's Kingdom have a clue what happen to her.

She was created by my magical powers, except for the gift what happens to be real.

Only to Coot.

And soon him to will live in my forest forever with me.

Wog.

The large beetle bug smiled within and walked behind Wog, back into the Dark forest.

Meanwhile at the Kingdom of Molive's Father, he was pacing back and forth in his chambers; wondering the whereabouts of his Queen, he knew of his daughters.

 The people of his land looked high and low, but to no avail she was found.

The King knew he needs help in finding his Queen and his daughter, who had been gone for over two Months.

 He couldn't tell the people of the land about him knowing the reason for his Daughter being missing.

He would have to reveal to them about her going to visit the old woman; in search of finding ways in destroying Coot.

His intense hate for the great Prince were causing him more problems he could handle.

Now what he's to do?

He sent messengers to Coot Father's Kingdom and other Kings Kingdom as well; he waited days on end for a response from them.

The King now knew hating someone at that depth, was not good at all, he know it's too late to take it back.

The damage is done.

Now he regretted allowing his daughter to help in destroying a man that he knew she wanted for herself.

He knew he had to tell the other Kings about the old woman that lives close to an unknown forest, one not even Coot and his band of hunters ever hunted in.

Coot was admiring his gift of the magical bow and arrows; as he looked at them he was feeling proud to be the only owner of such a magnificent gift.

His magical arrows always hit the target they were aimed at; then returned back to him to be placed back in the sheath which they came from. It didn't matter how many where shot; each one would return to Coot.

The magical gift made Coot more of brag too.

Laughing within, him alone through-out all the lands having magical arrows, to obey his command in slaying what-ever he choose to; never missing what he aim his arrow at

I no longer care if my Father disapproved of my special gift at all, the same applies to my Mother.

His band of hunters was very proud to hunt with such a man as Coot.

They had venture in another Forest, when news reached them about the missing

Queen and Princess, Coot's father and other Kings were summon to the Kingdom of Molive's Father.

Of all the Kings that was in his Kingdom. Coot's Father was the face he did not want to see; his intense hate for Coot, made it very hard to accept his Father's help.

The King was carrying so much guilt deep within his heart, just to look in his face he saw a mirror image of Coot.

The evil King was lost for words, when Coot's Father asked him, what can my people of my land and I do, in helping you find your Queen and Princess?

I vow to you I will do all I can, to help bring back the happiness to your Kingdom.

When Coot and his band of hunters returned they were shocked to see no great celebration was going on to welcome them home.

Only Sadness.

Coot asked the people; is this sadness about the missing Queen and Princess?

When he was told who the missing Queen and Princess were he hung his head, it hurted him more than the others, because he know of Molive more than the others did.

Coot asked the where about of his Father?

His Mother answered him by saying; your Father and other Kings are at the Kingdom of the missing Queen and Princess, to offer him their services in help finding them.

Coot turn to his band of hunters and said, we too shall go and aid in this matter.

His Mother did not approve of her Son's decision at all.

She asked him to wait until his Father return with his instructions of what to do.

His Mother was pleading with tears falling down her beautiful face. Coot told his Mother he's going anyway.

He ordered the people to clean their hunt and put it away until further notice, even the people of his Father's Kingdom was pleading with him not to leave.

To no avail Coot and his band of hunters turned and walked out the Palace never looking back.

Deep in the dark forest Wog had ordered some of its creatures, to stay close to the entrance to keep watch for Coot and the others.

Coot is the one I want most of all Wog said to them.

Thinking about having a man of his greatness living for-ever in my woods; is making me more happier when I think about it.

Especially when I think about him never seeing a human woman again long as he live.

Him for-ever living in my woods; will put a stop to all human women wanting his ass.

They would have to seek other human men, because Coot's ass will belong to me, Wog snickered.

Wog hated human men with a passion

Because it always wanted to be human; something that was not to be.

It is too evil to walk the Earth of mankind.

Wog was thinking of a method or some kind of trap to capture Coot; the trap it thought of was perfect.

It plan to tell Coot, the only way to get the human women back; he must hunt and slay a special kind of deer that roams deep in the dark forest.

Wog knew the killing of this deer would bewitch the person who killed it; into something so horrific no human eyes would want to look upon his face, a perfect look for Coot, especially when it comes to human women.

Wog wants Coot to remain with it forever hating humans same as it does; to rule beside it but not as powerful.

Wog feeling more evil than before was eagerly waiting for his special guest to arrive and become his friend after he's be witched.

Coot is to never know.

Wog was the one who helped him to be transformed into a monster that would hate and hunt men.

Coot and the others finally arrived at Molive's Father Kingdom; her father was shocked to see him there.

He had to change his evil feelings toward him; after all he needed his help in finding his Queen and daughter.

The other Kings felt honored that Coot was offering his help. Coot sat quietly and listen to what all the Kings were saying, King after King spoke.

Telling about what each of them had heard about the old woman of power that lives close to the dark forest.

One King spoke on the direction they need to go in search of this old woman of powers.

Coot began to feel un-easy about what he was hearing.

He wanted to hear more about this dark forest.

Of all his hunting, why he and his hunters never come cross it?

Somethings are not being told.

Coot was getting very agitated.

He asked Molive's father to tell everyone in the room everything and he better not to leave anything out.

The room was very quiet.

As he began to speak, he only looked at Coot's Father and said, for a very long time I envied your son.

I wanted my Kingdom to be the one that supplied the precious deer meat. So my Kingdom and land was powerful too.

But I knew I needed a son, instead I had only a daughter. That made me more envious of your Kingdom, so I began to plot in ways of destroying Coot.

Day after day night after night.

My daughter wanted Coot for her own and she also plotted with me; thinking if she was his bride, all the women of other lands would worship her by being his one and only.

But now things have changed.

My daughter left a while back with some of my men in search of this old woman of powers, to find a way in destroying Coot, her feelings were of this, if she couldn't have him for her own.

No woman will.

Now she and the others have not returned, and maybe my Queen is with them also. I fear something horrible has happen to all of them.

I have paid a very high price by having evil envy toward a person that has never wrong me or my daughter.

He just didn't want her for his bride.

Now I'm feeling she's to never marry or return home, my Queen included and the others.

I'm never to see my Queen or my daughter again; the King fell to his knees and sadly wept.

All the Kings and others were feeling sad for him.

Except Coot.

After the King revived himself Coot spoke out loud.

Listen to me Sir.

I never loved your daughter in a manner to make her think she was going to be my bride at all; she's the one that ask me. I asked her what part she didn't understand.

I don't want you to be the only one for the rest of my life!

Anyway!

I don't love you at all.

I only enjoy being in company with you; same as several other women of the lands; I said that to your daughter on many occasions Sir.

Believe me when I say, I never gave your daughter the impression that I plan ever to make her my bride.

Please do not let your heart believe it's my fault.

Coot said to the King, I will go on this quest in search of finding your Queen and daughter, but first you must tell me the direction I am to go.

Coot band of hunters refuse to go with him because they were afraid.

One told Coot, if the others haven't returned, the same could happen to us.

His remark irritated Coot some fierce.

Coot angrily said to him.

Did you forget they was being led by a woman?

When Molive's father heard those words from Coot he was livid.

He wanted to slay Coot on the spot.

But he held his temper.

After all he needs all the help he can get; he also felt if anyone could find his Queen and daughter.

Coot is the one.

The King asked Coot how many men he needs from his Kingdom. But the men in his Kingdom were afraid and resisted leaving.

Coot spoke and said, my men and me will go on this quest, if we don't return no one is to come looking for us, because that would mean we are dealing with a power not of this world.

Coot's Father ask, Son why you want to do this? It must be a very serious reason.

This man just told you (he was pointing at Molive's Father) he was jealous of your hunting skills and you not wanting to make his daughter your bride.

 Which caused her to conspire with him in finding a way to destroy you and now you are risking your life in finding this woman?

Tell me my son, what is your real reason for doing this?

Coot answered his Father by saying.

Father I am Coot, not you and Mother's Swoot, I am who I am, not meaning I don't love the two of you, because I love you all dearly.

I have to let this man know, hating me he was only hating himself, I'm going to give him a reason to not hate me anymore, the King hung his head in shame.

Coot explained to him, you are not the blame for people of the lands loving me the way some do. It's not anyone's fault that I am Coot.

I'm gifted from a higher power that does not apply to other men, I am the only one. The other Kings agreed with him because it was true in every word.

Coot's father did not agree with the other Kings at all, the thought of never seeing his son again, was too much for him to bare.

He's thinking how to convince his Son not to go on the Dam quest. His mind was playing tricks on him; evil began to build within him toward the evil king.

Sorrow of sadness showed on his once handsome face.

Coot mind was set on going on this quest, nothing was going to change it.

Not even the sadness he had brought up on his beloved Father.

The other Kings felt sadness for Coot's Father and Mother, they were lost for words, they would not approved; of their son going on a quest and they may never return home.

What a sacrifice for him to make.

And to think!

Coot!

Never loved the Dam woman.

Back in the dark forest Wog was very excited and eager to capture Coot. He had been planning for days how it was going to do it.

Deep in his woods roamed a beautiful white deer. It is the only one of its kind and harm was never to come to it for it is forbidden.

If anyone or anything captures this deer a terrible curse would befall on them.

The meat of this deer process everlasting life to any one that ate of it even its blood. Wog wasn't worried about having everlasting life at all, because it has live thousands of years anyway.

Death and it had agreed, long as it continue to cause evil among men it will forever live; only someone worthy of eating the meat of this enchanted deer, has the power to destroy Wog.

The evil beast knew all this; but how would Coot know once he's transformed?

Wog only thought it's a risk; it is willing to take.

Wog hated Coot more than any human man. He heard from the wind about him, not caring about any animals him and the others slayed.

Long there's a celebrated feast in their honor when they return to their home.

Now it's time for Coot to learn, he is not loved by Humans as he think.

Wog has no human women in its woods, only creatures he created from human men. Ghastly creatures of all kind living in tremendous amount of slime.

Wog slimy ass laughed within ; thinking about what his creatures looked like.

Things it know would not interest Coot at all.

Coot bid farewell to his Father and the other kings of the lands. He ask his father to tell the people of his land.

The ones that has loved him since his Birth; that he will forever love them too, especially most of the single beautiful young women.

Tell them when we return make sure it's the biggest celebrated feast since my

Birth; his father stood with tears running down his face.

He hugged Coot so tightly.

Thinking on how his gifted and skilled son, has made his Kingdom and his land the most powerful through-out all lands.

Now they are to be departed maybe forever.

Not knowing if we will ever see each other again?

A face that's a mirror image of my own?

His son was taking a love no other King or Father would ever feel; Yes his Parents named him Swoot; now the name he preferred to be call, proves he's really a Coot.

Besides being the greatest hunter of all in the lands, he's getting ready to prove to all.

How much of a Coot he is.

Molive's Father stood with his head hung low; feeling like a total dam dumb fool, the other Kings were thinking the same thoughts in their mind.

There stands A man, who hated Coot with a passion and now that same man, is about to go on a quest in finding his Queen and daughter; with no guarantees him or the others would ever return.

The other Kings told Molive's Father; if Coot and the others do not return, it would be on his head; and they would never come to his aid again.

!! NEVER!!

He would have to seek help from others.

Coots Father said to the sadden King.

If my Son and the others does not return and sadness befall my Queen and the people of my land!

I will declare WAR!

I give this Quest thing ninety days in rescuing your Queen and daughter. ! IF MY SON AND THE OTHERS DO NOT RETURN!

Your Kingdom and mine will be at war.

The other Kings were talking among each other, when one spoke and said, we agree with Coot's Father.

They don't return we will be at war with him against your Kingdom too, it's best you prepare yourself; get in touch with other Kings of other lands far and wide to aid you, if we have to go to war.

Coot's Father was searching his mind, how to tell his Queen about their Son's decision; he knew his Kingdom and the people of his land were going to be sad; until Coot and the others returned.

Molive's Father was not giving a dam about what was told to him from the other Kings.

Including Coot's Father.

His mind was telling him, the missing of his Queen and Daughter; gave him nothing to live for anymore, and far as the people of his land is concerned, having a new King is mostly what they want anyway.

The laws of my land my people never approved of them at all.

The King was thinking hard about the ninety days he's facing.

If Coot and the others do not return.

Him too would be missing.

Coot's Father was very quiet on his way back to his Kingdom; he was thinking about his son going on a quest in finding a King's Queen and daughter.

Someone that hated him with a passion and probably still do. Coot's Father tried to put all of it aside.

HE WAS CARRING A VERY SAD HEAVY HEART!

Tears began to run down his handsome face, thinking on never seeing his son again, asking himself questions.

How will or how can I go on never seeing my son again? Tears began to flow down his face once more. Thinking about the ninety days he has to face, with only hope to hold on to.

Days he knew would fly by fast.

Coot's father also was thinking about the words he said to the evil king.

War would be upon his land, if his Son and the others did not return home.

No one in his land would be spared, why should any one of his land live?

When they all knew of his evil plot to kill my precious Coot.

Coot's father yelled to the others.

!! STOP!!

They looked at each other wondering what is wrong. They watched Coot's father get off his horse and fell on bended knees, and spoke out loud.

Raised both hands to the open sky with more tears falling down his face.

He spoke to the God of protection, begging him to watch over and protect his son and the others, please guide them safely back home.

HEAR ME OH GREAT ONE!

Please let no harm befall them, hold them in your mighty arms of protection.

Please, Please, Please.

Guide them back home.

MIGHTY GREAT ONE!.

You grant me this request.

I WILL GIVE YOU MY SOUL!

It was no sign from the great one; it only starts to rain very hard. Coot's father knew the rain was a sign.

Letting him know.

His son and the others foot prints were being washed away, never to walk the path that would bring them home again.

Still on bended knees the others looked at their king, and noticed how quickly he had aged. Never to have the look of his beloved son again, the mirror image of him was no longer, all remained were the look of a very sad old man.

His men picked their king up to his feet.

Thinking within, from this rainy day, and days to come, joy and happiness will never be in their land again.

The most important ray of sunshine will never brighten the kingdom or the land.

NOW IT'S A TALE OF SORROW.

Their loved and skillful hunter will never hunt for the kingdom or land again.

How can our king go on, and try to pick up the pieces of what's left?.

War is only ninety days away, depending on Coot's and the others return.

Being at war?

Is it going to bring Coot's and the others back?

Sad to say.

No one at the kingdom or the land, will ever set eyes on Coot or the others again.

Meanwhile Coot and the others were getting close to the dark forest. Coot instructed his men to stay close together and pay close attention to what's in front and behind them.

His gifted bow and arrows remained close and at his reach. It began to get very dark, his men were afraid.

Coot calmed their fears by showing them his bravery, and behold, right in front of them was the entrance into the dark forest.

They saw trees tall as mountains, never had any of them seen trees that tall before, including Coot.

They heard voices that didn't sound if they were human.

Voices of eerie sounds.

They clung much closer to Coot, because he showed no sign of being afraid at all.

Suddenly something moved.

Only Coot caught sight of it. It was a very large white deer, a color he had never saw in all his hunting.

The beauty of the White deer won his heart, his only thoughts were to capture it, and never will the others know what he saw.

This is to be his prize alone.

Coot thought he heard the trees whispering, something that could never be.

Trees talking?

Coot's only thoughts, that it was the sound of the wind, until the others heard the voices too. One of them was swiped up by a branch from one of the trees.

He was so afraid he couldn't utter a sound. Later, when it was known he was missing, only Coot spoke.

He told the others.

We are not alone.

He cautioned them once more to remain close to each other.

Then a very eerie abnormal cry was heard. The trees began to speak out loud to them.

Saying.

An evil is headed this way, to capture the human man it's been waiting for over a thousand years.

Coot showing no fear at all, stood firmly in front of one tall tree, and angrily asked it.

Where is my other dam companion?

Tell me now tree!

If you don't!

You and the others will be tree stumps.

Very quietly his hunter was placed gently with Coot and the others, unharmed and very happy to be back with them.

One tree told Coot, you and your companions have venture into a forest that no human men has ventured in thousands of years. You and your companions are never to return to your homes again.

The evil one that lives deep in this dark forest, it's been waiting for a human man as you,

COOT.

Tell me tree how you know so much about what this evil thing wants, and then tell me how you know my name.

Coot asked it?

To say you are only tall trees that provide shade from the heat of the sun.

SUDDENLY.

The trees had faces.

But only one spoke to Coot and his band of very frighten hunters. We do not only provide shade from the Sun, but try to warn mankind about the evil one that dwells deep in this dark forest.

Now we cannot help any of you unless you want us too. Coot asked the tree, why haven't something destroyed this evil thing before now?

You trees alone could've done something, besides standing tall every day.

Three of you could handle the thing, unless it's more powerful than you are telling us, or maybe none of you knows about the power it process.

The trees was quiet as they listen to Coot rant about all of them being cowards, allowing an evil thing to rule the forest, and all it want is a human man, which happens to be him.

After Coot finish ranting, the tree spoke once more. Let me try to explain things to you great hunters.

This forest is bewitched by this evil thing, but it only has power deep in this forest, only when men venture deeper the thing can control them.

It have things that will help it to have power over the men that venture there, and one is they are never to return to see daylight again.

What this so call evil thing has; that some men willing to live in this dark spooky-ass place for-ever.

Tell me tree?

Precious jewels that's buried deep in the dirt.

Enough!

Coot angrily said to the tree!

My hunters will destroy anything that brings harm to any of us.

The tree said to Coot; you still don't understand great hunter, the wind whispered your name above all other men.

The evil one only wants you, the others will be slaves to it and you.

Maybe so, Coot said with sarcasm.

But this thing must face me and mines, I'm only here to find the women that venture in this place, so tell me trees any of you warned these women of this evil thing?

Great hunter no women ever venture here, the thing hates human women. They are useless to him. It only want human men, and you great hunter it wants most of all.

Tell me tree, why this thing wants only me?

Because it wants to be like you, but it can't and never will, the evil he process is very intense, and that alone makes it want you even more.

Especially hearing about your way with human women, something it will never get the pleasure of enjoying.

Is this thing human Coot asked?

NO!

And it will never be.

Coot grunted and said, Fuck that thing!

Meanwhile Coot's Father and the others made it back to his kingdom. He was met by his Queen. The look on his face told her what she didn't want to ask.

But she did anyway.

Where is my Son?

He reached out his arms to her. She lay in his chest and asked him softly.

We are never to see his face again she sadly asked?

They both cried, because they knew it was true. She looked in her king's face now old and sad.

Turned away from him and slowly walked to their balcony, it happen so quickly, she couldn't think about living in the world with-out her handsome Son.

Coot's father knew living with-out his Queen and Son; his days will be long and empty, so he too jumped.

A kingdom destroyed.

Because of a love one that will not be there anymore. The people of the kingdom and land had no ruler; another king will rule the richest kingdom and land,

Only for a while.

According for the new king to remain rich, first he needs a skillful hunter as Coot, someone he would never get.

 Majority of the men of the land despised Coot and didn't give a shit about his band of hunters.

The new king that became ruler change many laws.

The first one was; no eating of deer meat, anyone caught eating of the meat will surely be put to death.

All the people were ordered not to speak the word deer; it too will be punishable by death.

CHAPTER 2.

Meanwhile back in the dark forest.

Coot let his hunters sleep, so he could slip away to hunt for the Beautiful white deer that laid heavy on his mind. By some magical spell he saw it.

STANDING SO PROUD!

Something else was with it standing quietly behind Coot. He heard it speaking softly to him saying, Kill the white deer.

You and the others will be taking back to your land everlasting life. Coot asked the voice, are you the evil thing that dwells in this Forest?

NO!

The evil is those trees your companion is resting on their branches, I am here to help set you all free from this forest.

What about the two women and men that ventured here? Did you help set them free too? Coot asked the voice again.

DID YOU HELP SET THEM FREE?

No women or men been here, maybe they went to another forest.

The voice changed the subject, saying to Coot, slay the deer and all your questions will be answered.

Killing of the deer and eating of its raw flesh; will give everlasting life to all people in your land; other people will die off in other lands. What a wonderful gift to give the people of your land.

Coot remembered the words that were told to him by the tree. About not being able to leave the forest at the entrance.

The tree asked Coot to dig at the bottom of it, and take one of the green stones that's buried in the dirt. When they are in the presence of this evil thing, not to make any bargains with it; never tell it anything at all; just keep walking forward.

Coot mind began to reflect on the whole conversation he held with the tree, especially learning its name, which is Kapier.

Telling him and the others when humans visit the forest thousands of years ago, until the evil thing came there, causing no sunlight to ever shine in the forest again.

Coot began to realize the wrong he had done, leaving his band of loyal hunters resting on the branches of trees; that now are their friends.

Tall beautiful trees that warned and told him about this evil thing that wants only him and his hunters would be turned into slaves.

Coot thought how the other trees were so happy to have humans resting on their branches again.

But No!

He wanted to slay the beautiful white deer alone. Now he's to face this evil thing alone too.

Also remembering the words from his hunters, asking him to rest also. The sight of the white deer had capture his heart.

He wanted it for himself.

Even though he was told the deer is the only one of its kind (white).

And it only showed up once every hundred years; to eat of the rare figs that grew there. Remembering asking Kapier about other hunters that hunted there, to be told the animals in the dark forest roamed free, it was no need of their meat like other deer's him and his hunters hunted.

Many deer's of this forest have beautiful colors of fur.

The voice brought Coot out of his thoughts, still telling him to slay the white deer. Him wanting the deer so badly; he removed one of his magical arrows and placed it upon his bow; getting ready to let the arrow flow, the green stone began to shine very brightly, the voice yelled.

Throw it into the air!

That tree is trying to trap you!

Coot let his magical arrow flow.

The beautiful white deer fell, as always the arrow return to Coot. He slowly turns around to see where the voice is coming from. Coot could not believe the horrible sight that had been standing behind him.

Behind him stood a big green slimy block of ugliness, a thing with ten eyes and one gigantic eye in the middle of its face with a horn on top of its head.

Twenty arms of different lengths and legs, feet made of claws. Yes it was a horrific sight to behold.

Coot told the beast.

You tricked me.

That tree was my friend.

You wanted to slay that deer, now since you did; you will be forever with me in my forest, by the way great hunter.

My name is Wog.

I already know of you Coot, Wog snickered.

Coot looked at the slain deer that happen to be still breathing.

It called out to him.

Coot rushed to the deer; the deer was no longer the color of white but dark grey. The deer asked Coot to come closer.

When he did the deer spoke and said. I am the last of my kind. You will never hunt deer again, but I will still help you, lean down and drink of my blood; after drinking of the deer's blood.

The deer spoke again saying to Coot; now you will know the reason you are never to hunt deer again.

Coot realized he was standing in a bright blue light, his magical bow and arrows blended into him, never to be used by him again.

Coot was no longer a man; he was half deer, no fingers or feet only claw hooves, his eyes turned to giant diamonds, antlers on his head, he even had a little short bop tail.

Wog was watching and loving it all.

Coot began to shake his large head; he tried to scream, to only sound of a weak horn. The green stone remained on the forest floor.

Wog picked up the stone and threw it into the dark air with one of its long arms. It was very quiet for a few minutes.

Now sits another thing, a very large Deer-man; dazed and very confused. Wog was proud of his evil ugly ass.

His plan worked out perfectly in capturing Coot. Now to explain to the deer-man his purpose and why he will remain for-ever in the dark forest.

Coot was heavily breathing.

Wog asked him to relax he is there to help him, and protect him from the ones that are trying to harm him.

Coot stood on his legs, as if he's still a man. Wog did not like that at all; he wanted Coot to remain on all four's as other deer's.

Rather he's on all fours or not; he still was a horrific sight to be looked upon.

Wog loved that even more.

Coot asked Wog.

Who's trying to harm me?

Humans Wog answered.

Coot told Wog something his evil ass didn't want to hear.

My name is Coot, I am the greatest hunter in all the lands; my Father's kingdom is the grandest of all other Kingdoms, I am loved by all.

Wog said, Not anymore.

This forest is your home now.

Forever!

Come Coot let me show you the beauty of your new home Wog said to him. Let me remind you of something that's important.

Yes your name is Coot, look in the water in front of you and tell me what image is looking back at you.

Meanwhile back at the entrance of the dark forest, Coot's band of hunters had waken from their long nap. They were asking Kapier where's Coot? Sadly Kapier had to tell them everything.

The hunters listen to every word spoken, until one of them spoke out loud, telling Kapier.

It doesn't matter!

We are still going to look for him!

If that evil thing wants to keep living in this forest, his best bet is not to cross the eight of us!

Coot is not the same man anymore Kapier sadly told them. Why you sound so sad one asked him?

Kapier said to them; when you all look for Coot; never look behind you; walk straight ahead.

If you all hear the sound of your beloved hunter's voice; only say to him, you all is heading back home.

Remember do not look behind you.

Kapier was silent, he spoke no more.

The hunters were feeling afraid; they did not have the protection or bravery anymore. Coot was not with them. They had to be brave on their own.

They bid Kapier Farwell; the walk through the forest was very scary, they heard all kind of eerie sounds that didn't sound human at all.

But they continue walking staying close together. Then they heard the sound of a weak horn. They thinking it' the sound of hunters; so they walked toward the sound; but behind them was no other hunters.

Something was hunting them.

Being afraid the hunters forgot what Kapier had told them; they looked behind them; and saw a large 12ft tall monsters deer, that spoke to them with the same voice as Coot.

Bargains were made.

The hunters did as they were told by the monster. Coot's faithful hunters were never to know who was behind or helped them to become the now ghastly creatures.

That's to be at Wog's command; and serve him as slaves and the deer-man too.

Coot blocked his mind not to think of them as his loyal hunters at all, only ghastly creatures that would be his slaves in his woods

Chapter Three.

The trees were whispering about the approaching human; it had been one hundred years since a human came to the forest.

They were so happy.

The man thought he heard voices of other men; so he decided to answer back by saying

! Hello!

A voice said! Hello and Welcome!

The man was frightened.

He never seen a tree move or talk before; the tree convinced him not to be afraid of them, no harm will be fall him at all; the man looked up at the trees; never had he seen trees tall as them before.

He spoke to one of them, and his fear went away. The tree asked, what brings you to this forest?

 The man said, I'm here to gather some of the rare figs; that's said to be in this forest.

My wife have a craving for them some fierce; a tree spoke up and said; those figs are deeper in this forest; way deep.

If you venture deeper in this forest; you will come across Coot who's a very mean deer; I'm not afraid of no deer the man said laughing heartily; the tree said Oh No! My new human friend!

Coot is more than just a deer!

Much more.

If you come across it; please do not bargain with it by all means; because he's going to try. We can help you not to fall into Coot's trap; but you must promise us you will do as we say.

 All I come here for is the rare figs; not no dealings with some wild deer; my wife is expecting our first child, and the rare figs is what she's craving for.

Anyway, tell me tree; how would this Coot know that I'm in this forest? He have spies keeping watch?

Coot already knows you are here my new human friend; the sound you heard of a weak horn was him.

He's waiting for you to venture deeper in his woods; then he will approach you.

I'm sorry!

My name is Kapier.

The only way to escape Coot; is a green stone that's buried in the dirt beneath me; dig beneath me now and get one stone; it will protect you from Coot.

After the stone was removed from the dirt; Kapier asked the man, what is your name my new human friend?

My name is O'Dea.

Kapier asked O'Dea to listen to him very carefully; and he will explain the purpose of the green stone.

The stone that you are holding in your hand will protect you from Coot; long as you don't bargain with him for any reason.

When you get the rare figs; do not let Coot bargain with you about anything; do not take of the diamonds that will be in your path only take the rare figs.

Then take the stone and throw it over your left shoulder; a path will appear before you; that would lead you out the forest.

Coot will not be able to harm you; his powers are only in his woods; sunlight cause his powers to weaken; if you do it differently from what I'm telling you;

You will fall under Coot's spell.

But come my friend and rest your-self on my branch and talk with us before you journey back into the sunlight;

The other trees were saying to each other; how happy they would feel if a human was resting

On one of their branches too; suddenly the sound of a weak horn was heard once more. Kapier told O'Dea, Coot is letting us know he knows you are here.

O'Dea said I'm not afraid of Coot, long as I have this stone; Kapier told him and long as you remember what I told you also.

O'Dea was enjoying resting on the soft branch of Kapier; as he talked with the other trees too.

He was showing them his beautiful bow and arrows; and telling them of all the animals he had slain with them.

He talked once more about his wife expecting their first born child; and the reason he come to the forest.

Why the wind do not blow in this forest? Where are the birds, flowers, and please tell me why you the trees are so tall?

A tree spoke and said; it's an evil thing dwells here and been here for thousands of years; it only wants this forest dark and creepy; to have it any other way; it will lose its powers.

Please tell me my friends; why you all so tall? Kapier spoke for the others; reason we are tall as we are; bring us closer to sunlight; something this forest do not have anymore.

 The evil thing that dwells here glad we are tall as we are; reason it don't come close to the entrance of this forest; it come years ago and haven't been this way since; are you all afraid of this evil thing and Coot?

No!

Kapier angrily said!

The evil thing powers are not strong as they are deep in his woods; if it come close to the entrance ; it powers weakens.

That help keep us safe from it and Coot too.

What happen to others that venture in this forest Kapier?

I'm going to tell you a story of long ago; once a very skillful hunter and his band of hunters come to this forest; in search of a Queen and Princess plus the people that was traveling with them.

This great hunter caught sight of a very beautiful white deer; not caring that this deer was the last of its kind; the hunter slayed the deer; even after he was warned not to slay it; the evil thing that dwells deeper in these woods.

Wanted this great hunter to rule alongside it; but he wouldn't be as powerful; this great hunter is the one that's waiting for you.

He's Coot!

The evil thing name is Wog.

Coot not knowing the beast had been waiting for him a long time; so Wog set a trap to capture him; now it has Coot; Wog helped to bewitch Coot into a monster more horrible than it.

Now Coot is waiting for you to venture deeper in his woods; O'Dea interrupted Kapier, asking him ; any other hunters tried to kill this evil thing and Coot?

No!

We never heard from them again.

If they had taken our advice; maybe they would had found a way to destroy Wog; then Coot would not be a hunter of men at all.

O'Dea thanked Kapier and the others for advising him in not being weak to fall for Coot's trap to capture him, to become another ghastly creature to slave for him and Wog.

The other trees reminded him again; not to take anything from Coot, and not to look behind him at all.

Because he would be offered all kinds of great things; just get the figs and leave the diamonds , gold coins where they lay.

Because that's Coots way of entrapping you; get the figs throw the stone over your left shoulder, and leave this forest.

Train many men as you can and return back and destroy Wog and Coot once and for all time.

Remember my human friend, Coot will try to stop you from getting to the path that will lead you out of this forest.

What he has to offer more greater than diamonds and gold coins O'Dea asked Kapier?

The trees said to him; we are not permitted to say anymore; you have to decide for yourself what's more important.

Please do as we have told you; rest now my friend Kapier asked. Morning is near.

The following morning O'Dea bid Farwell to his friends; he started on his path in getting the rare figs; remembering not to look behind him at all; he kept walking forward; then he saw the figs; they were huge and juicy; he had no idea they would be that huge; all he could carry amounted to four.

Lying next to the figs was a huge diamond; he saw another one and many others and gold coins too.

He remembered what Kapier warned him about Coot's trap; he refused to touch any of them; then he heard the sound of a man's voice. The voice was saying to him.

Every woman loves diamonds; just think how many women you can choose; by giving them even a small one.

You can have any woman you choose; O'Dea told the voice behind him; I have the woman of my choosing.

She's my wife and she's expecting our first child; look in front of you the voice behind him asked.

Hanging from a tree was a large bag filled with gold coins; lots of them.

O'Dea was thinking about how grand him and his wife could live; he almost looked behind him; but something else was in front of him; another large bag containing diamonds of the largest size.

Even more on his path in front of him; the man's voice was still behind him telling how rich him and his wife could live for-ever.

O'Dea almost looked back; he placed his hand inside one of his pockets and felt the green stone.

He pulled it out and was about to throw it over his left shoulder as he had been instructed by Kapier.

When the voice spoke again.

If you take the diamonds and gold coins; your wife and you would be rich forever; O'Dea asked the voice; are you Coot?

Yes!

Now turn around and face me.

Looking at the diamonds and gold coins once more.

O'Dea.

Asked the voice, tell me what price I would have to pay besides my life; if I turn and face you?

Quietly the Voice said.

Your child.

Why my child O'Dea asked?

Giving me your child; is the only way to grant you and your wife immortality and very rich too.

O'Dea was thinking about what had been told to him from Coot; living forever and rich too; my wife and I can have more children.

! Wait !

What about the child; will my unborn have immortality too?

What if my wife and I have more children, does the same apply to them too?

! Yes!

O'Dea was thinking about it all.

Slowly he dropped the green stone; turned and faced Coot; standing in front of him; was this gigantic beast standing as a man, but had the looks of a deer.

It had antlers, claw fingers and feet, big diamonds for each eye, fangs on each side of its mouth, covered in gray fur with a bop tail.

What a ghastly horrible sight.

O'Dea was so frighten; he hung his head from the sight of looking at the monster; most men would had fell dead looking upon me Coot said to O'Dea.

The diamonds and gold coins helped him forget the sight of Coot a little.

Are you ready to live for-ever human?

O'Dea nodded his head and said yes; Coot picked up the green stone from the dirt; and threw it in the dark air; a loud cry could be heard in a distance.

 Your tree friend Kapier is no longer able to save you now; take many diamonds and gold coins you can carry; remember human man the deal you and I made;

O'Dea asked again. What about my unborn child?

You mean my child worthless human!

When the child is born; you will bring it here Coot pointed and lay it upon this golden bed.

O'Dea hung his head being ashamed of the deal he had made with a monster; if I do not give you my child; tell me what would you do to me?

Kapier has told me you cannot return to sunlight; Coot laughed out loud and told him; I don't think you want to anger me human; then

Coot fell on all fours.

O'Dea was really frighten from what he was looking at.

Coot turn to a worst kind of monster; froth was forming at his mouth, his eyes were no longer diamonds; they became red as blood and he began to grow larger.

He asked O'Dea, tell me human would you want something as this to hunt you and kill everybody in my way?

Trying to get to you.

Think about it as you are standing here; in front of me frighten close to death.

No Coot!

I wouldn't want any other to look upon something as horrible looking as you.

O'Dea was getting ready to leave; when Coot reminded him about the rare figs; something he had totally for gotten about,

Being greedy grabbing diamonds and gold coins.

Coot looked at him with disgust; watching him grabbing the jewels.

O'Dea was thinking he has to find a way in explaining things to his wife.

Whenever you want more of the jewels; this is the path you would take; even when you bring the child to me.

Never bring anyone with you, especially a woman; you are to always come alone;

this is the only path you are to use when you want to enter.

Coot waved his clawed fingers and the path to the outside world appeared crystal clear.

Remember Human always come alone; even when you bring my child.

I will be waiting!

Coot went back into the forest; all was left was the scent from him.

The way out was in front of O'Dea.

He was loaded down with the precious jewels and only four figs.

Chapter Four.

When O'Dea made it to his home; his wife was eagerly waiting for him.

What took you so long she asked? You had me worried, did you come cross trouble in that forest?

No! I did not have any trouble.

Besides.

One day is not long my wife.

You been gone more than one day; how about you been gone a week.

O'Dea had no idea he been gone that long.

Did you get the figs she asked him?

Yes!

He was so happy to give them to her; when he pulled out one of the figs; a gigantic diamond was stuck to it; his wife really screamed; saying I have always wanted a diamond.

Now I have both, a diamond and the rare figs too.

Where did you get the diamond my husband?

Her husband was feeling if she wanted the diamond more than getting the rare figs.

After his wife had calm down; he asked her to sit on his lap and he would tell her everything that happen in the dark forest a week ago.

After he finish telling his wife what happen; he showed her more diamonds and gold coins; forgetting about the other three rare figs.

Sadly she asked her husband; our unborn child belongs to a beast in that dark forest?

I'm not giving my child to a beast.

O'Dea tried to explain to her they had no choice but to oblige to the beast.

I already taken diamonds and gold coins from it; plus I can get plenty more and we will live forever being wealthy.

We will have more children that will never grow old and die nor shall we.

They held each other and wept; but oh how rich they were; people of the land was wondering where their wealth suddenly come from; when they were some the poorest of all in their land.

O'Dea was now the richest man in all the land.

But his wife kept a very sad look on her face.

In time their child was born.

O'Dea knew he had to give the baby up; he was thinking about it all.

His beautiful new born daughter belongs to a beast that lives in that dark forest.

O'DEA tried all he could to please his wife.

But it was to no avail.

O'Dea picked up his beautiful new born daughter and held her close; took a beautiful blanket wrapped the baby in it.

His wife was pleading and begging him not to take their child to a beast that lives in such a dark place.

He only looked at his wife and walked out their front door; his wife got out of bed; still weak from childbirth and followed him.

She had no knowing of where he was going; the scent from her baby she could smell her; the hope in getting her baby back; helped her to keep going forward and not feeling any kind of fear.

Suddenly she heard voices.

Right in front of her she saw the monster and her husband; it was not as ugly as she had thought; a large deer but stood if he was a man; even built as a man; the antlers and fur didn't matter even his bop tail.

She saw her husband bowing down to this monster; as he was presenting their child to it.

The monster was telling her husband; remember you are never to come here trying to get this child back; only come to get the jewels that's here and nothing more.

Our deal is not to be broken Coot reminded O'Dea.

The child is mine forever.

Will this child live forever also Coot?

Yes! Coot laughed out loud!

This child will live forever; when it grows it will be my slave forever too!

The mother had heard enough!

My baby will never grow to be your slave the mother screamed.

You ugly ass beast!

The sight of Coot seeing a woman!

He turned into something more horrifying to look upon.

Now he really was a monster!

The fangs in his mouth grew longer, he fell on all fours and turned into this horrible thing.

Coot was spitting froth from his mouth; asking O'Dea.

Why you brought this woman with you here?

No human woman has ever seen me; now she must die. O'Dea was pleading with Coot to spare his wife's life.

What must I do to keep you from killing her?

Please tell me?

The only way I would spare her worthless life; she has to be blind forever; not to remember what I look like to tell others. Especially other women.

Do you mean my wife is never to

See daylight again?

Not only never to see daylight; she will never speak again neither; that is my final offer or I will kill her worthless ass now!

O'Dea continue to plead with Coot.

OK!

Worthless man!

Your woman will be able to see for one year, not speak but see; after the end of that year darkness she will return.

Now leave me before I change my mind and kill both of you.

Unknown to Coot as he travel back to his mansion in his woods; the baby had been watching him .

She never utter a sound to be a new born, nor did she cry to be fed.

Back at O'Dea's home; he still was pleading with his wife to look at him, even though she couldn't speak.

He was promising her; he's going to get their daughter back from Coot; even if it cost him his life.

He talk with her about the year to come; when she will lose her eye sight.

His wife stood and slapped O'Dea hard across his face; causing his nose to bleed heavily; then went to her bedroom.

Because she refuse to sleep in the same bed with O'Dea ever again.

The diamonds and gold coins didn't mean shit to her anymore; the absent of her only child and her being given to a monster.

That lives in the dark forest was more than she could bare; thinking about how her husband let greed; cause unbearable unhappiness for the rest of her life.

All mattered to her was rescuing her only child from a monster name Coot.

No one her husband know has the power of time to help him destroy Coot.

Her husband!

He's only interested in getting more of the jewels that's helping him to continue be extremely wealthy forever.

Coot is the happy one.

Of all the bargains he had made with men over a hundred years; none had ever given up a girl child before. It were only preteen boys young as 19yrs, still he made slaves out their Fathers too..

Now this is a very special bargain.

Coot changed every time he looked upon the sleeping child; how am I he going to care for her? Who can I trust that will be willing to help me?

Creatures in his woods were ghastly looking; not a one was fit to care for this beautiful child. He start thinking it's time to feed this child; I cannot forget she's a new born.

I have to find someone to care for her soon; or I would have a dead child on my hands real soon too.

There is one creature Coot trusted.

When he was transform in to this monster; the creature remained at his side and still do.

The creature also knew of Coot's parents; that's been dead so long ago; never to be in this world again; tears flooded his eyes.

His only concern now is to bring his girl-child so she can be cared for, like cleaned and fed.

Coot had the perfect ghastly creature in mind; now to get to it quickly as possible.

Coot also has to bring the child deeper in the woods were majority of the diamonds and gold coins rested in his dirt.

And to meet Wog's slimy ass.

Something he's really regretting.

Wog and Coot been friends for over a hundred years, well not close friends; just two ghastly beast that rules the deeper part of the forest.

Coot really despise his evil ugly ass.

Never had the two come cross a human girl child before; mostly of their ghastly looking creatures were men of long ago.

Now they are Wog's and Coot's slaves to work sun-up and sun-down; digging the precious jewels in the dirt; these men from long ago had also venture in Wog's dark forest.

Now never would any of them is to return to the Sunlight or their homes.

Only if they had done what Kapier and the other friendly trees had advised them.

! HOW SAD !.

Coot was thinking on how much he has to plead with Wog in keeping his girl-child; the only plan he thought might work.

Is to convince Wog, once the girl-child grow she will slave for the two of them for-ever.

Maybe Wog would believe me.

The baby remained quiet; never did she cry about anything; only smiled each time she looked at Coot.

Maybe this is the girl-child Wog mention about; telling me of a girl child so many years ago that's destiny to destroy his slimly evil-ass for-ever.

All the male children they had taken; no father ever tried to get them back; but this is a girl child and her Father might be thinking differently about rescuing her;

Then again the fathers were never told they sons will live for-ever neither; this girl-child was told to her father that she's to live for-ever with me in my woods.

Coot arrived at the extremely slimly home of Wog.

All the years he's visit this gigantic slime ball; he never liked it at all; slime would be all over, even on his food.

The most disgusting of it all.

Slime be hanging out of all Wog eyes and where-ever it stand or sit; slime would be left behind.

Coot presented the girl-child to Wog; he only sniffed and said.

This is a human girl child; and this worthless child must die tonight'

No Wog!

Think about when she's grown up; she can slave for both of us; his evil ass thought about having a female slave in his woods.

Only to be treated worse than the other ghastly creatures he created.

Coot pulled the blanket from the child's face; Wog looked at her and said.

Such a shame.

This beautiful girl-child is to grow to live as a slave and no human will ever look upon her face. I want to kill her now.

The baby turns and looked at Coot and smiled.

He had never saw a smile as hers in a hundred years from any female.

His heart began to soften.

Now he only wanted the baby for himself; not for Wog and the others to mistreat.

Coot began to plot again.

Meanwhile back at O'Dea's house; he also was plotting on how to get his baby back from Coot's ass.

Him being a very wealthy man; he offered large sums of money; to anyone with information concerning the dark forest.

He assured his wife once more; he's getting their baby back; she has to have trust and faith in him doing so; his wife ignored him again.

The years went by fast.

Twenty years and no one come forward with information concerning the dark forest; O'Dea's wife still blind, deaf and dumb.

But she remained young and very beautiful.

Majority of the people in the land; had grown old and died off.

Many had no memory of the years gone by; many had for gotten about the events of long ago.

Hard times had fallen on the land old and ruin; food was very low for many.

But at O'Dea's home food was very plentiful.

People come far and wide to buy food from him; some had to give up their homes and land to buy food for their families.

To keep from starving to death.

Still no information about the dark forest was mention at all.

One day out of nowhere.

A woman paid O'Dea a visit to his grand home; she informed him she knows about this dark forest; she also had venture there; she said to him.

 At first I thought it was a myth talked about by men; especially when I was a tot; O'Dea asked her; tell me what make you think now it's not a myth.

The woman said; I will only speak of this forest if we are alone.

That is the only way I will tell you; what I know about this forest.

O'Dea went into a deep thought.

All the men in this land never come forward with Shit about that forest; now stand before me A Woman?

He knew he had to take chances any way he could in getting his child back from Coot; depending on if his daughter is still alive after all these years.

Then again the woman might know something after all.

O'Dea asked her to follow him.

The woman walked pass his beautiful wife; sadness was upon her face; she wanted to speak to her; but decided not to.

O'Dea brought her to this beautiful room that was down in a cellar of his grand home.

No other ears will hear what you about to say to me; are you sure Sir she asked?

Yes I'm sure O'Dea assured her!

The woman began to tell him.

Ten years ago my father venture in that dark forest; searching for the rare figs that were told that grows there; and to this day he's never returned.

My only brother and other men in our land went to that forest to look for him; they too has never returned; my mother paid large sums of money in trying to find them to no avail they haven't been found to this day.

I made a vow to my mother; that I will find them.

I feel sorry for your mother O'Dea sadly told her.

Still you haven't told me what I need to hear about the forest that's interested to me.

She began to tell him things about the forest only him remembered; about no wind blows there, flowers don't grow, birds not in trees, and how tall the trees are.

No hunter is permitted to hunt there; because some had killed all the animals that once roam free in the forest.

It is known of this evil thing that lives there; but it lives way deep in the forest that happens to be a

    Monster!

O'Dea hung his head in shame; thinking how he gave his only child to Coot from being greedy; and wanting to be rich and live for-ever.

knowing Coot told him to come alone; reason why his beautiful wife is to remain blind, deaf and dumb.

Now he's trying and willing to spend large amounts of money to make up for that guilt.

O'Dea's greedy guilty ass.

He was spending large sums of money; still coming to dead ends with nothing, concerning information about the dark forest.

O'Dea asked the woman had she seen or heard about any others that venture in the forest besides her father and brother.

Yes!

But them too has not returned; that's when I decided to venture there alone; me wanting to find my Father and brother helped me in not being afraid.

When was your last visit to the forest O'Dea asked out of concern.

Yesterday!

I goes often as I can in search of my father, brother and the others.

I still can't find them .

Have you ever saw the trees move or talk O'Dea asked?

No!

The river is all that spoke to me.

Where you afraid when you heard the river speak, O'Dea asked her?

No I wasn't afraid at all; the river became my friend; it even gave me a gift.

What kind of gift O'Dea asked?

The river gave me this.

O'Dea was in awe!

In her hand was a green stone.

The same green stone his tree friend Kapier had given him long ago to protect him from Coot. He had to get that stone back.

He began to feel very desperate in getting the green stone from her. O'Dea calmed himself and ask.

How much will you take for the stone?

I can never part from this stone; it's my only way in finding my father, brother and my other people.

O'Dea wanted the stone badly.

I been warned by my river friend; not to let go of this stone to anyone she replied.

O'Dea was even more desperate to get the stone.

Woman!

I know you are called by a name.

What is your name?

Dar is my name.

Tell me Dar.

Have you ever heard the name Coot?

Yes! I heard of his name from my river friend; I also was told; Coot will never look upon a woman at all.

Did your river friend tell you why O'Dea asked?

No! Dar responded.

What about the young woman you spoke of earlier?

The young woman I saw; her eyes were covered and she was being led; with a gold chain around her neck by a ghastly looking creature.

O'Dea was in a rage; thinking about his beautiful daughter in darkness with a chain around her neck; being led by some ghastly creature in the dark forest.

COOT MUST BE DESTROYED!

What land are you from O'Dea asked?

I am from the land where the Sun, Moon and stars rest for one year; all is left is darkness night and day.

The men of my land have it very hard during that year to hunt and keep our families fed; my reason for being here at your home; to bargain with you for food for my people.

Why are you alone Dar?

How much food can one woman carry to feed several people in your land?

The question O'Dea asked her; she went silent thinking the same.

Yes how could she?

O'Dea said to Dar.

Give me the green stone and I will make sure the people in your land never be hungry again.

Only the stone will guarantee it.

I ask you again O'Dea said to her; why no men in your land venture here with you to help carry food depending on you getting any?

Only men left in my land are old and sarded not enough strength to lift heavy loads; our women care for them; especially the ones that don't have wives or daughters.

 The women will never leave the old men to defend for themselves; once upon a time they were protectors of us.

Follow me O'Dea asked Dar.

She was brought to another gigantic room; in that room was so much food; it looked if it could feed many tens of thousands of people in many lands.

I have hundreds of room as this one O'Dea bragged.

Give me the green stone and one of the rooms can be for your people and much more.

Give me the stone!

O'Dea's guards stood aside and Dar looked around the gigantic room which was fill from top to bottom with delicious foods of every kind.

Food she knew would be plenty for all the people in her land.

O'Dea showed Dar a room that held abundance of gold coins and diamonds; enough to make her land very rich.

NO! Dar screamed!

Only give me the food I earned; telling you about what I know concerning the dark forest; O'Dea took her back to the room where the food was.

O'Dea asked her, tell me Dar, did your river friend speak of a tree name Kaiper?

The river never spoke of this tree, but others did she answered him.

I was told to look for the tree; but to no avail I could find it; all the trees looked the same tall and unfriendly.

Not one of them gave me a whisper; even though I was told from the river they all could talk.

O'Dea was thinking.

Maybe my old friend is still standing tall in the forest; I really need that green stone from that woman; killing her to get it will cause serious problems for me and my home.

It has to be taken another way from that Bitch!

Dar's voice brought O'Dea out of his evil thoughts; explaining to him the green stone is no use too him; the power of the stone is for her alone in finding her love ones.

O'Dea was willing to give it another try in getting the green stone; he notice his wife trying to feel her way in to the room with him and Dar; his guards stood aside never assisting her at all.

How sad she looked.

Once a very out-spoken woman; that live each day of her life being happy and in love with her husband, awaiting their first born child.

Now she's one sad sight to behold; blind, deaf and dumb and very un-happy; all because her husband wanted to be rich and live for-ever; even the price of giving up their only child in doing so.

Dar touched her on the hand and tears fell from her eyes.

Your wife is very Beautiful Sir.

Tell Me.

Did you marry her in that condition?

Or some kind of evil bewitched her?

Never mind my wife's condition; my only concern is you giving me the stone.

Your wife and the young woman I saw in the dark forest has the same look about them; a look if they can be twins; you wanting this stone.

Tell me Sir.

Do it has anything to do with the young woman in the forest?

No!

The stone is a jewel, one I never saw of its kind; that's my only reason for wanting it; I showed you many rooms of my home; that's filled with diamonds and gold coins; not one is the color of the green stone at all.

So tell me Dar.

You are willing to remain poor because of one stone; that can make you and your people rich for-ever?

O'Dea hung his head in shame; knowing deep within he done the same; giving up his only child and the reason his beautiful wife; is to suffer in her pitiful state forever .

His greed had cost him all that would had made him really and truthfully happy.

Now he want it back.

But How?

Dar reminded him again of the food she's earned for her people.

After all.

She did provide him with information about the dark forest.

O'Dea called out to two of his guards; to help her load food to take to the people of her land.

I would had given you much more; if you had given me the stone O'Dea said to Dar. If I hear or see more concerning the dark forest. I will return to you for more food with the information also.

O'Dea sent two of his trusted men to help her with the loads of food that were on carts with wheels.

Also another man went along also as a spy.

He is to report back to O'Dea all he can about the land Dar lives on; his guard was instructed to make sure he is unknown to the others.

After the food is unloaded when they are headed back to the land.

Kill them.

Bury their bodies in unmarked graves.

People of this land is not to know anything.

Chapter Four.

Wog had a meeting in his woods with some of his trusted ghastly creatures.

It was about Coot and his now grown human woman. Wog felt he's protecting her from him and the others.

Remember long ago Coot stated when the then girl-child gets older, she would be a slave for us all.

Now it seems if he's only letting the worthless Bitch slave for him only. The others agreed with Wog.

It's time for her to come here and slave for us.

All agreed except one.

A little one-eyed toad-man.

That once slaved at Coot's mansion, and was treated very badly by him. He was to work every day and half the nights, the little one-eyed toad man knew how mean Coot was.

Now to think about the beautiful human woman being his slave brought tears from his only eye, it made him even sadder to think of her coming there to slave for Wog and the others.

To live her life in slime!

Slime on her food!

Slime on her body!

And she's never to be clean at all.

She would be hungry and beaten at times, just because she's a slave.

At least Coot is only mean and never has beaten her as he has beaten me. The only reason he keeps her in darkness, he don't want her to see his face.

She may be in chains but they are made of pure gold.

The little one-eyed toad man was thinking of a way becoming her friend; without the other creatures knowing about it.

He know he has to be very careful, because Coot couldn't stand the sight of him at all.

Wog decided to visit Coot's mansion.

He know not to enter it.

Coot did not like how he left slime over everything he touched.

Plus he was a loud mouth!

COOT! COOT! COOT! Wog yelled out.

The creatures in Coot's mansion put their claws in their ears to help quiet down the sound from Wog's loud slimy mouth.

Coot come to his golden porch and asked Wog.

! What The Fuck You Want Slime-ball ?

Now that's not a respectful way to treat your guest Coot.

I'm here on business.

I want you to explain to me, why that human woman haven't come to my woods and slave for me and mines?

After all these years she's only been here in your neck of the woods.

Tell me why?

When you brought her to me as a baby girl-child; I wanted to let some of the others eat her that very same night. But you pleaded with me not to and I spared her worthless life.

Because you told me once she grows up, she would slave for both of us and to this day she haven't been in my woods since that night.

So tell me Coot.

Is she your slave or our slave?

Do you have a dislike for me and mines and don't want her in my woods at all?

The creatures at Coot's mansion had stop doing their work and gathered with him on his golden porch.

One had the human woman with it. She was dressed and very clean, but her eyes were covered with a silk blindfold.

Wog was very dis-pleased at what he saw.

Coot told the others to go back and continue with their work. The woman was snatched back inside and sadly weeping.

Wog was pleased to hear the sound of her weeping. He yelled to Coot's creature.

Make Her Weep Again !

Yes Do It Again!

Coot yelled to his creatures.

She's a slave don't you all for-get that.

Slaves only for you

Huh Coot?

So tell me when our slave coming to my swamp and slave for me?

Dar made it back to her land, her Mother was very glad to see her so was the people. They was helping unload the tons of food.

Her Mother wanted to know about the men that came with her. Mr. O'Dea sent them with me because I was alone and needed help bringing the food back; she told her Mother.

Many questions were asked from the people. Dar main concern was the feeding of the old and the children. Then men that come with her felt sadness for all of them.

Exception of one.

The Spy!

He had a job to do.

Dar was telling her Mother about O'Dea's wife. How sad she looked and being blind, deaf and dumb, but very beautiful.

Dar's Mother showed no compassion about what was being told concerning O'Dea's wife.

I'm happy and bless that you made it back safe my precious daughter. I don't give a dam about O'Dea or his wife.

Mother do you have a dislike for O'Dea?

Yes I do !

Because I remember what he did long ago; tell me Mother Dar asked?

OK I will her mother responded.

Long ago his wife was expecting their first child; to this day no one has ever saw or heard about the child; it was told by many he left the child in that dark forest never to be seen again.

That's the reason his wife refuse to see, speak or hear.

What he did with their daughter is the reason why, and it's something else too.

Neither he or she has aged at all, all the people that lived long ago in his land has grown old and died; but yet they remain young and free of any kind of sickness.

I was the age of five when I heard my parents talked about him leaving their baby in that dark forest.

My parents been dead over forty years; now I'm close to their age and O'Dea and his wife still look the age of their late twenties?

Never go there for food again.

We will find another way of getting food when this food gets low. He's given you enough food to aid people of other lands. It must be something he wants from you or something he wants you to do.

My guess.

It's something to do with the dark forest. Did you tell him of you venturing in that forest in search of your father and brother?

Tell me Dar!

Did you?

Yes Mother I did.

It was the only way he would have given us food.

Dar was confused what her Mother said about O'Dea leaving his only child in the dark forest; as if he gave it as a sacrifice for some un-know reason.

She went to her room to rest from her long journey back home. Thinking about her father and brother.

If only they were here.

Things would be much better for everyone in the land.

O'Dea's spy was close by.

He had heard the whole conversation

All he had to do is wait, and wait he did.

After he had killed the other two men.

Not caring about their families that were waiting for them to return home.

Anything to please O'Dea in receiving diamonds and gold coins.

Still not enough to make him wealthy though.

Only enough to keep him and his family from being hungry. Killing him or robbing is out of the question; too many loyal and faithful others around him.

O'Dea was in deep thought in getting the green stone from Dar at all cost. Then go to the dark forest and look for his tree friend Kapier; to help him in getting his now grown daughter from Coot's half deer ass.

But he know he had to be very careful in doing it. He decided to wait until his faithful guard return with news about Dar and her people.

He put his sad wife to bed; and he too fell asleep; to be waken by his guard that went with Dar back to her land.

First O'Dea wanted to know if he killed the other two men.

Yes he was told.

What manner were they killed?

Boss I took my sword and cut them into several pieces and scattered their remains.

Leaving them for the wild animals that roam in her land to feast on.

Many ferocious animals roam freely in that land.

O'Dea asked his guard why he seem so happy about what he's done.

I'm not happy about killing of them; I'm happy about the present I have for you.

I'm eagerly glad what I'm about to give you Boss. O'Dea asked him to come to the parlor. After he was seated he ask his guard.

Show me my prize?

In his guard's hand laid the green stone!

O'Dea was beside himself.

He almost snatched the stone from his guard's hand.

He next asked, how did you get it?

His guard explain everything to him in saying.

The woman puts the stone in a black jar with the lid tighten; the stone shines into a very bright light as the sun, that bright light puts her into a very deep sleep.

I still can't believe how easy it was for me to get it. The stone also spoke to me; saying it has no power for me at all.

I told the stone I don't need anything from you, my boss provide me with everything I need.

I put it away.

Because I didn't want the stone speaking to me anymore.

Then it turned green again.

O'Dea told his guard never speak of this to no one; come with me O'Dea asked his guard; he was taken to one of his gold rooms where he gave his guard one hundred gold coins.

(Cheap un-grateful bastard).

Now O'Dea has the green stone.

Plus his evil ass had the spy killed and took back the gold coins.

he wasn't taking chances with anyone; knowing of him having the green stone.

He's only thinking going back to the dark forest and rescue his daughter; from Coot's ass once and for all.

The green stone was place in a jar.

O'Dea made sure the lid was tight as he could tighten it. The stone refuse to shine a light at all.

It remained green.

O'Dea began thinking the stone had no powers for him also.

He laid down and fell asleep.

The stone began to shine as he slept.

Only to cause his wife to dream of her daughter. O'Dea began to dream also; he dreamed of hearing his daughter calling out to him.

He tried to grab her from Coot.

His daughter was riding upon Coot's back; he was no longer half deer and man; he was a golden deer with wings.

He was telling O'Dea.

You will never get your daughter back.

She will love and live with me for-ever in my woods never return to the world of men.

O'Dea woke from his dream sweating some fierce.

He heard his wife crying out loud; she was crying for her daughter; pleading to the unknown to see her face just once. O'Dea shook his wife awake; in awe that she was speaking again.

He asked his wife what she meant; she wants to see their daughter's face once last time?

O'Dea was very happy to hear his wife's voice once more; he asked her could she see and hear?

Of course I can Idiot!

She angrily replied.

I am speaking, seeing and hearing you very well. O'Dea not wanting to upset her any more quietly asked her.

How can this be?

His wife asked him to listen to her very closely.

For twenty years I've been praying to a powerful voice; saying to this voice I told it.

I don't want to live rich and for-ever; my only wish is to see my daughters face, place kisses on her jaws, hug her, tell her how much she's love by me still.

O'Dea spoke and said.

Wife remember Coot said our daughter and the two of us is to live young, rich and for-ever.

But our daughter is to live with him for-ever in his woods.

No!..

His wife screamed!

That monster only spoke those words to you; when he was given our child.

NEVER!

Were the words spoken to me at all!

The voice come to me long ago and asked me to keep silent about it; I was to remain blind, deaf and speechless and always remained sad.

And one day I would be whole again and happy.

Did the voice tell you its name O'Dea asked?

YES!.

The voice said he's called Kapier.

Did the voice mention to you about a stone?

O'Dea knew he had to tell his wife everything that happened in the dark forest long ago; letting her know he had met Kapier.

 Telling him about Coot before he ventured deeper in the forest in search of the rare figs.

After he confessed to his wife of everything; she asked him.

 Why didn't you listen to him O'Dea?

I will tell you why.

Your greed for riches were too much for you to resist, instead you gave that monster our only child; and not to mention the torture I had to endure.

That monster is never to be seen by eyes of a woman or women at all; to say our daughter is now a young woman.

 But the voice of Kapier assured me for years, our daughter is not being harmed only pretending to be; Coot let the other ghastly creatures he trust take care of her.

Suddenly the stone began to shine a bright light; O'Dea's wife looked into it, a voice was telling her to go into the light.

She Did so.

There in the light of the stone, she saw her beautiful daughter.

Her Mother went to her and placed a kiss on each jaw with plenty hugs of joy; she turned away from the light of the stone and went to O'Dea.

She walked up to O'Dea and slapped his ass hard across his face; as she done years ago leaving a bloody nose once again.

Today is your last time calling me by the name of wife!

I will be called by the name given to me at Birth.

Armiee!

Then his wife turned very old and died.

The light from the stone was gone too.

Coot!

Tricked me once more O'Dea was thinking.

If my wife can pray to die.

So can I.

Not until I face Coot and kill his evil ugly-ass once and for all. O'Dea now know it's his daughter that's to live for-ever; to live for-ever with Coot.

Back in the dark forest, the little one-eye toad man was being worked by the others very hard doing many hard tasks.

He was close to dropping dead from being worked. The other ghastly creatures were not caring at all, about the hard work he's doing for them.

Wog enjoyed it more than the other creatures how the little one eyed toad-man was being worked.

His evil ugly slimy ass worked him even harder while laughing with the others.

A ghastly creature crawled through the slime and said.

Master Wog.

Another human woman been in the forest and some believe Coot let her in and helped her to leave.

Maybe his thoughts of being with human women is starting to surface after all these years. He might be trying to become a human man again.

I need to send one of you to be a spy at his mansion Wog said. Then we will know for sure if he's really one of us.

Chapter Five.

Wog found out Coot was not aware of the human woman that had been in the forest. The creature that told him was torture and killed for telling him without having proof.

The little one eyed toad-man was happy the creature was now dead, the torture and pain he suffered from it for years. Now he's waiting for another creature to take its place to continue on with his suffering.

The little toad-man was praying to the un-known for something; to release him from the harsh treatment from Wog and the other evil creatures that lived in his slimy woods.

Wog decided to pay Coot another visit.

But he was not to know of it.

When he got to Coot's mansion; he saw the human woman on her knees, feeling around and washing Coot's claw feet; he was pulling her hair causing her to fall over.

Wog loved the sight of it.

He was happy to see Coot being mean to her; he heard her begging Coot to remove the rags from her eyes (they were not rags, but made of pure silk) she was pushed to the ground!

Coot stood on one of her legs and said

Never speak to me again!

You are not allowed to speak at all; when I find the one who taught you how to speak.

It will truly die!

She began to weep once more.

Wog was beside him-self, he wanted to make her cry even more.

Coot smelled him and looked up.

He knew he was being watched by Wog; but he pretended as not.

Come over my friend and watch my slave obey her master.

So!

 Wog said.

You only has one human woman slave?

Where is the other one?

What the hell you mean the other one slime-ball?

The other woman that's been in your woods Wog told him.

You mean Man don't you?

 No!.

 Wog said.

A woman!

Coot begin to think back.

The only woman came to his woods was O'Dea's wife. But she's blind and can't speak, no other woman been in his woods since according to him.

Wog is trying to trick me for some unknown reason; I will only let him talk of this other woman; because I have no idea what other woman he's talking about.

Wog made it clear to Coot another woman had been in his woods.

Coot went to his woman slave and pull roughly on her hair and asked. Who you been talking with behind my back?

Tell me now!

No one master! No one!

Wog slimy ass wanted to pull her hair and make her cry even harder! And call him master too.

It was a sad sight to see a beautiful woman pleading, begging and crying to a beast; with gold chains hanging from her neck; if they were a noose; that she's to be led by if she was an animal.

Coot yelled to the creatures of his mansion.

Come get my slave and lock her in the dark room and remember not to remove the band from her eyes.

Water and no food!

Be gone all of you!

Wog and I need to talk alone!

No interruptions!

Coot looked at Wog with disgust. He was standing in a puddle of slime, all his eyes had slime hanging from them and the gigantic eye that was in the middle of its head ;tremendous amount of slime was hanging from it.

Wog knew he was not permitted to come any closer to Coots mansion.

 His slime is the reason why.

Coot was still in dis-belief that bulk of slimy Shit was his friend.

 When they was alone Coot asked his slimy-ass.

Tell me how you know another woman has been in my woods Wog? Then tell me who told you.

I never smelt the presence of another human woman at all. You been had and lied to my slimy friend. Remember the creatures in your swamp were once men too.

You have a king and prince, father and son in your swamp; until you transformed them to the ghastly creatures they been for several years.

Maybe you Wog is being betrayed.

It don't matter Coot he replied; you are to capture this woman. I never hunted women.

Only men!

You must find this woman Coot and destroy her; if you don't succeed our powers will be worthless.

Remember when I told you about the only way I can be destroyed?

It will take a human woman of pure kindness to destroy me for-ever.

Including you.

My reason long ago wanting you to destroy your now grown human woman. The only way we are safe from her; is to keep her a slave, blind, and never to speak.

At one time I thought you was keeping her for your-self; to remind you of when you were a man.

With most of the woman in your land wanting you above all the other men.

Coot assured Wog.

Never!

My feelings for human don't exist anymore. None of the people in my land long ago; they did not make not one attempt; in finding me or the others.

Wog did not believe one word said from Coot.

After all it wasn't too long ago he was a human too.

Wog told Coot it's time for him to be headed back to his swamp; he has a one eyed toad that need a beating; for being a useless one eyed toad. Coot laughed out loud and said to Wog

Farwell my friend.

Unknowing to Coot.

Wog had left a large beetle bug-man at Coot's golden mansion to spy.

Back in the land of Dar; she left her land a very angry woman; someone had stolen the green stone; she knew the only place the stone could be found.

At the home of O'Dea's!

When she made it to his home she was inform he was not there nor his sad wife.

O'Dea was headed to the dark forest with plenty armed men; his only thought rescuing his daughter from Coot. Him having the green stone made him more brave.

No longer he's afraid of Coot!

He took the path Coot had told him many years ago; when he wanted more of the precious jewels.

When they entered the forest the path was before them; his guards were amazed of the riches in front of them.

Large diamonds and gold coins were sparkling all over their path. In all their minds they were thinking on being very wealthy men themselves.

O'Dea instructed them all; do not touch any of the jewels. It was very hard for the men to obey his words; looking at the jewels some wanted to slay O'Dea, gather many jewels as they could; return to their land and being very wealthy forever.

O'Dea reminded the men once more.

 To put out of their heads about taking any of the jewel that's laying on the forest floor before them.

 To dis-obey his command can result in death for each one who take of the jewels. Some of the men was willing to take the risk by them having little to live on anyway.

They resisted the temptation of touching any of the jewels and obeyed O'Dea's command; walking down the path in the forest many more jewels were seen by them; riches beyond their wildest dreams.

The men were looking at how tall the trees were and became afraid; one said, let us leave this place I feel evil around us; a feel of black power is in this place. O'Dea assured each of them.

I have something in my possession that has power of its own; what I have will protect us from any kind of evil that lives here.

You all must trust me O'Dea said to them.

As they entered deeper in the forest O'Dea instructed them to stay close to each other; no one is to wander off alone.

O'Dea was not afraid.

Suddenly they heard the sound of a weak horn; only O'Dea knew about it; a sound he's never to forget.

Coot once again is letting them know he's aware of them being in his woods. The sound began to get louder.

When some of the men looked behind them; the face they saw was not Coot; it was the angry face of

Dar!

She had close to twenty men with her.

Give me the stone she demanded of O'Dea!

Bitch!

Go back to you land!

You don't want to fuck with me!

Many years I've waited to confront the monster that lives in these woods, and his ugly-ass will be confronted and kill today!

The stone have no powers for you to use against no monster in these woods; the power of the stone is only help to me; in finding my Father and Brother Dar tried to explain to O'Dea.

Bitch! You don't understand!

The stone that's in my keep!

Its power within has killed my wife; that alone means this stone owe me a great debt.

O'Dea listen to me Dar asked?

Maybe the two of us can work together and benefit from the stone's power together; I'm not leaving this forest without finding my family Dar pleaded.

My problem with Coot has to be known about today, O'Dea was thinking within.

LISTEN TO ME ALL OF YOU, O'DEA SHOUTED!

He began to tell them the story of long ago.

After the finishing of his story; now they all know about his missing daughter.

But none of the others were aware that Coot is half man and deer.

O'Dea made sure of not telling any of them; then he decided to tell them.

WAIT!

There's more!

This monster name Coot, is half man and deer.

Now!

Dar and the others did not know what to say or do; they all began to question

O'Dea. Asking him is he sure the stone he's holding; have the power to conquer and kill a monster as Coot?

Tell me O'Dea one man asked?

You ever saw or talked to the monster that lives in this forest face to face? Or you heard it from others?

We all need to know what the monster of this forest really look like; none of us really know if you are being truthful or you only telling us this shit.

So you alone can get the jewels for yourself and continue being the richest man in our land.

Don't be stupid Idiots!

O'Dea snapped.

We must go deeper in his woods; only then Coot will appear; he knows we are here anyway.

 Remember stay close to each other and never touch the jewels in your path; doing so each of you will remain in this dark place for-ever.

As ghastly slaves.

Maybe this monster Coot is responsible for the missing of my Father and Brother Dar was thinking.

O'Dea was very pleased to have many men that's ready to go on the hunt in the forest, to seek and find Coot and destroy his ass for-ever. It will be a very happy day.

Him freeing his daughter after so many years; living in the dark forest with Coot and his other ghastly creatures.

Chapter Six.

Meanwhile back at Coot's mansion a meeting was being held also.

Only among his slaves.

No longer they wants to slave for his evil mean ass anymore.

Including Wog's slimy ass!

The beetle bug was the only one that was not at the meeting; he was keeping watch on Coots' every move.

Especially his human woman slave.

The beetle bug watched Coot go to a golden door; he moved closer to listen to Coot speak to who-ever was behind the door.

 Come out worthless human woman !

The beetle bug was in awe!

When it saw a beautiful human woman standing in her door-way; he heard Coot call to her again; she refuse to take a step out of her door.

Refusing to obey him.

He told her again.

Then he looked closer.

Coot saw her lips moving.

She was praying!

He began to ask himself.

 Who taught her how to Pray?

Someone in my mansion has betrayed me.

Coot was very angry.

He has to find the one or ones that did it.

He put his clawed hoofs over her mouth to stop her from praying anymore; she began to weep so sadly. Coot took her by the hand and walked her out of her room.

The beetle bug was watching still.

Coot sat her on a large diamond and asked her.

Tell me who taught you how to pray.

The same one who taught me how to walk, talk, feed and clean myself too, she replied.

Master I also has heard you speak to a power to help make you whole again; so now I pray to this power to be released from darkness; so I can look upon your face.

Coot enormous diamond eyes looked at her; only thinking how beautiful she is; but for her to see his face; he knew the sight of it would frighten her; its best she continue to only hear his voice.

A tear fell from one of his enormous diamond eyes.

Remembering long ago.

Several women was at his feet trying to get his attention. Now women is never to look him in the face again.

Never !

The beetle bug moved closer.

Trying to see and hear much more.

Coot sniffed the scent of it!

Before the bug could move!

Coot had it held high off the forest dirt!

Speak!

Or I will crush the life out of you with this (showing the bug his other clawed hand).

The bug began to speak with fear in its voice.

Wog left me here to spy on you!

If I don't return to his swamp in three days; others would be sent here to destroy you and all your others too.

Especially your human woman slave!

Tell me worthless useless bug.

What the others look like that's coming to my woods to kill me and mines?

You better not lie!

Others that look like me the bug told Coot.

Tell me bug?

Why Wog wants to spy and destroy me and mines?

Wog thinks you know about the other human woman that's been in your woods; and you want both of them to slave for you only.

Tell me bug, is there more I need to know about Wog's plans in destroying me?

Yes Coot there is more!

Wog plan to take the human woman and let her slave in his swamp; after he kill you and yours off; then he would have the dark forest back under his command alone.

How Wog plans to take her Coot laughed?

That's his reason for leaving me here; to help find a way in doing it.

Well bug!

Wog has one less spy now!

Coot crushed the beetle bug between his large claw fingers; until life was out of it.

He put the crushed bug in a large glass jar with a very tight lid and buried it beneath the dirt; went to his human woman and said to her.

Remember you heard nothing!

She only sadly wept.

Back in Wog's swamp he was eagerly waiting for the large beetle bug to return; when it did not return after four days.

Wog began to wonder if it too had, joined up with Coot and the others in his woods.

Only time would tell, Wog was thinking.

Standing in slime the little one eyed toad-man had heard it all; he was thinking of a way to get to Coots woods and tell him everything Wog is planning; only thing , how would he be able to convince Coot he's on his side?

Knowing Coot can't stand the sight of him at all.

Is still worth to try?

The little toad-man decided to slip away from Wog's swamp; many years he's been in slime and filth; now it's time for him to be free of his miserable life in Wog's swamp.

By trying to go and convince Coot and help save the human woman from being Wog's slave in his slimy swamp for-ever or as long as she live.

Which wouldn't be long?

Wog and several of his ghastly creatures were eating in his slimy quarters; talking about how they are going to kill Coot and all his slaves in his woods.

The little toad-man made sure plenty of food was at their disposal; giving him enough time to slip away and not being missed until their food was low again.

That would give him enough time to reach Coot woods; even though Coot was evil and mean (when he slave for him long ago) his woods are livable with no sign of slime anywhere (only when Wog visited)

The little toad-man hadn't been out of Wog's swamp for many years; but he remembered how to get to Coot's woods easily.

One of Wog's guards was sleeping when it should had been keeping watch. The little toad-man slipped past it fast as he could.

 If he had been seen out of Wog's slimy mansion, he would had been torture some fierce; his only thought getting to Coot and telling him about Wog's plan; even if it cost him his life.

 HALT !

The little toad-man was cornered!

Four guards of Wog had been watching him all alone; one grabbed him and asked.

 Why you not at the mansion?

Master Wog know you out her wondering around?

 Answer me slave !

The poor little toad-man was so frighten.

HE FAINTED!

Wog guards drugged him back to the slimy mansion and locked him in a dark slimy room; then headed to Wog's eating quarters to report what had happen.

Back in the dark forest O'Dea and the others including Dar; agreed Coot must be destroyed once and for all; only then the forest will be restored with the beauty it once had.

What none of them didn't know; another monster is the real reason why the forest no longer is beautiful; none of them knew about Wog's evil slimy ass.

O'Dea promised Dar he would return the stone to her after he rescues his daughter and kill Coot. Dar was trying to explain to O'Dea, the stone has no power for him at all.

Suddenly the trees start making loud noises; O'Dea remembered his first day being in the forest long ago; the trees at the entrance are the only ones that could speak.

But they had venture deeper in the forest and the trees there were letting Coot know they are in his woods.

Back at Wog's swamp he had his final meeting with his ghastly creatures; after he was told about the little toad-man wandering out-side his slimy mansion with-out permission.

The others were surprise; when Wog didn't order some to torture and beat him; he only told him; your one-eyed ass will be worked until you falls dead.

Wog then turned to the others to continue with his meeting; of course the little toad-man was not to attend, he was only a slave.

But it did not stop the little toad-man from listening closely at the slimy closed door. (Reader close your eyes and vision Slime!)

Wog's plan is to take the human woman from Coot; bring her to his swamp to slave only for him. Pretending; telling his ghastly creatures she would slave for them too. Some of his creatures wanted his mansion and woods too; let him be the same as the other deer's that roam in the forest, eating grass, nuts and the rare figs.

No my friends Wog laughed!

He's more than an animal.

 Much more.

And that alone cause him misery.

Why are you so fond of Coot one asked?

When we take the human woman from his ass; ask me again Wog snickered.

Then we will know, if he hate humans as he pretends.

All the others were agreeing and laughing with Wog's decision; the little toad-man had tears in his eyes; thinking if Wog succeed in taking the human woman from Coot!

That would prove to the others, including him how powerful Wog really is.

The battle in the dark forest is about to begin.

Dar wants to find her Father and Brother.

O'Dea wants to rescue his daughter from Coot; she's the only one he has in the world.

Coot wants to keep his human woman for him only.

Wog wants to take the woman from Coot.

The creatures in Wog swamp wants his woods, mansion and his slaves.

The little toad-man wants freedom to only rest from the hardship he's endured from Coot, Wog and the other ghastly evil creatures in the forest.

Coot locked his human woman in another room with a golden door. Then he headed out to Wog's swamp.

O'Dea told Dar he's the one to slay Coot and maybe then the stone would help him; but the stone remained quiet.

Wog instructed the others not to interfere with him slaying Coot; he wants to slay him alone.

Wog , however had no intentions of killing Coot at all; it was only pretending to the others.

Why kill my only friend?

It is I who helped him to be transformed into the monster he is; but he's never to know it was me.

Coot think it were the trees at the entrance that tricked him long ago; including his band of hunters; that he killed himself after being bewitched by that white deer, he wanted to slay with instruction from me.

Wog left his with his ghastly creatures from his swamp; headed to the woods of Coot; leaving a trail of slime from them all.

Back at his slimy mansion, the little toad-man were glad they were gone; at least he would be able to rest; didn't matter to him at all he was locked inside. Rest from working is all he desired.

O'Dea and the others were still walking down the same path, diamonds and gold coins continue to be all over same as when they first entered.

O'Dea asked them to stop and go no further.

Something is not right he said to them. We been walking hours and Coot has not appeared at all.

Why are we stopping Dar asked?

Think about what I'm getting ready to tell each of you O'Dea said to them.

The path has not come to an end yet; longer we walk, longer the path become; we are not going to take another step on this path.

Instead!

I want each of you to open up a bag and start picking the jewels from the forest dirt; lay your bow and arrows down.

Pick up many jewels you can carry.

The others were too happy to get the riches, including Dar. Coot was not thought about at all.

Only the jewels.

Until they heard the sound of a loud weak horn.

O'Dea knew it was Coot for sure that time.

Because he sense others that didn't live in his woods were taking his jewels.

O'Dea knew the taking of his jewels would bring him to them very quickly; something Coot would really destroy them for; his jewels were the only way he trapped human men; after he tries to bargain with them; only to be turned in to ghastly creatures in his wood; only to slave for him for-ever.

The trees were calm once again.

O'Dea stood and watched how the others were grabbing the jewels like maggots eating shit; for-getting what they come to the forest to do.

The sound of a weak horn was heard again; O'Dea knew for sure it was Coot.

He know of them in his woods taking his jewels; Dar asked, tell me O'Dea, why you not getting some of the riches that's laying before you?

You are not being afraid are you?

Look around you O'Dea?

We are close to one hundred strong; with this many armed men we can destroy Coot and many others that look like him; come now and get your share of the jewels with us.

 O'Dea refuse to answer her at all.

He continued looking at all the greed that was around him; thinking long ago he too had been greedy; the reason he have his greedy-ass in the forest; trying to make amends for it; by rescuing his daughter and the dying of his wife.

O'Dea took his horn from his side and blew into it hard as he could; the only way he could get the others to pay him attention.

Dar's men only obeyed her.

She waved her hand to them and immeadally they stopped gathering the jewels, stood to her attention.

Un-knowing to all.

Coot had been watching them. But he was alone. No way he could conquer those many men; he need help in doing so.

Then he saw Dar.

Memories of long ago start to surface from within; remembering of the years gone by; him being catered to by beautiful women as she.

Now he's a monster!

Something he knew. Looking at a monster as him would frighten her to death; All men that come with Dar; had no way of knowing what was standing in the mist of them; was a twelve ft. half man and deer watching them all.

Including O'Dea's army of men.

Back in Wog's swamp he reminded his ghastly creatures once more.

I am to slay Coot!

Master Wog?

Why you want's to slay Coot?

Letting one of us kill his ass; you can stand back and watch.

Wouldn't that make you happy!

NO!

Wog screamed.

All of you have your orders; to dis-obey me will cause each one of you; anger from me even death; now get your-selves ready to destroy the humans that has venture in my woods.

THE BEGINNG OF THE END.

The sound of a weak horn was heard by all once more.

SUDDENLY!

They all saw it!

Standing above them all.

A gigantic deer-man.

They all were frozen with fear!

Coot stood with Golden wings on his back spread open in great splendor; he began to grow taller, his diamond eyes began to glitter; his fanged teeth had froth dripping from them; his clawed fingers and feet were longer and looked of sharp razors.

The green stone in O'Dea's hand start to shine very brightly.

Then it began to speak out loud.

I am the power that lives within this magical stone; I have been watching and listening to all of you.

The bright light from the stone; shined its light on Coot.

You long ago were a great and skillful hunter; plus a prince of the greatest kingdom in all the lands; you were loved by your parents and all the people in your land; plus other lands too.

You wanted to be above all men when it came to women.

Knowing you didn't care for them as you should have; out of guilt you and your band of hunters; went on a quest in finding A Queen and Princess.

Not knowing of the evil thing that was waiting to capture you; a trap was set and you fell for it.

Out of Greed!

You and your hunters were warned about this evil thing that dwell deep in this forest.

Did you take heed in this warning?

NO!

Your ego alone made you stupid.

I will tell you something of importance Coot.

Your parents jumped to their deaths; because they didn't want to live in this world with-out you being part of it.

Coot remained still.

The bright light from the green stone had him captivated and locked within it; the stone continue speaking to Coot.

The evil thing that's been your friend for over a hundred years; is headed this way in pretense to his other ghastly creatures to kill you.

But it only wants to kill the humans; the evil thing wants you to live with it forever.

The evil thing you know as Wog.

Is the one that helped you to be transformed into the monster you are, and hater of human men.

Remain still the stone ordered Coot.

The stone commanded Coot to listen very carefully as it continues to speak..

Coot did remain still.

The stone shined its light upon O'Dea.

Foolish man!

You too were warned.

But you also refuse to listen; instead you bargain with the monster that stands above us all; greed was your reason.

Then after several years.

You thought you were tricked by this monster that stands above us.

NO!

You did that to yourself.

With help from Greed.

Something you were willing to give your only child for; another price you had to endure from your greed.

The misery your wife had to endure for the longest time; you known for years what you had done; now you are here to try and take back.

 What never should have been given at all?

You too remain still.

 And think about the hardship you caused your own ass.

The light from the green stone blinked twice and shined on Dar.

You wanted the strength of a man; thinking it would help bring favor to your father's eyes; therefore you became envious of your only brother; wishing evil befall him so your father would have no choice but to favor you; now you too here; trying to find the whereabouts of them.

If you find them.

It will bring back peace and happiness to your Mother and the people of your land.

Your Father not being there; your people don't have a ruler, and your Mother must choose from some of the men; in your land to rule beside her.

Remain Still Foolish envious Woman!

The light from the stone was brighter.

It shined on everyone.

Listen to me!

All of you the stone shouted!

Evil for all mankind is headed this way.

Unite together!

Kill this evil thing and its creatures!

They looked at each other.

Including Coot.

Stone!

Am I to ever remain this way Coot asked?

The light from the stone did not shine anymore; it was a plain green stone again; the voice from it did not speak anymore.

Coot stood above the others.

They were so frighten!

None tried to destroy him.

Only looking to Dar and O'Dea in what to do.

Loud eerie sounds were being heard by all; Coot pointed up to the sky and asked them.

LOOK!

Standing before all of them were tall trees; one picked up O'Dea with its branch and said to him.

It is me my human friend!

Kapier!

We are here to help you.

O'Dea bowed his head in shame.

Hold your head up my friend.

I forgive you!

Kapier looked at Coot.

You are forgiven too he said.

No!

I am not to be forgiven at all O'Dea said to Kapier.

You don't know what I have done!

My greed helped in the dying of my wife and giving my only child to the monster that stands above us all.

No my human friend!

Your wife is alive!

She has been safe with us.

Because she is the only human woman to see Coot as the beast he is.

Now it's two.

Your wife seeing him.

Helped saved her.

What about the rest of us my friend O'Dea asked?

Joined together and destroy what's coming your way.

I will help too!

Coot loudly spoked!

Dar and her men agreed to help also; deep in O'Dea's pocket the green stone shined a very small streak of light on Coot.

Kapier asked Dar to rest on one of his friends branches; this is not the kind of battle for a woman; come he said sit with Armiee.

After this day Sunlight will return to the forest; birds will nest here again; blooming of beautiful flowers will be all over this forest; men shall hunt once again; kids shall come here to play once more.

How happy my friends and I would be to have a young boy to climb our limbs once more.

A chilling scream was heard!

Everyone!

Stay calm Coot ordered!

As Coot spoke he was transforming once more.

The large diamonds were no longer his eyes, no antlers, claw fingers and feet, no fangs!

Not even his little bop tail.

Before them all stood.

The great hunter of long ago.

Coot reached behind his back and felt his prized bow and arrows.

He was happy once again!

Now standing for all to see!

Coot the man!

Everyone was in awe, including Dar; Kapier said to him; welcome back great hunter, welcome back.

I will kill this evil thing Coot boasted.

All of you stand back!

How can you alone kill this thing great hunter O'Dea asked?

You will need help killing his ghastly creatures we heard about.

No great hunter let us help in destroying this evil thing with you.

NO!

This thing name Wog.

Owe me a debt Coot angrily said.

Now it's getting ready to face the real Coot; not the monster he helped me to become long ago; Dar and O'Dea's men did as they were ordered by Coot; they sat down if they were little boys listening to their teacher if they were in a class room.

He took one of his prized arrows from the sheath; placed it upon his bow.

On bended knee he waited for Wog and the others to emerge from the dark.

EEEEEEEEEEEEEE! EEEEEEEEEEE! EEEEEEEEE! Was all could be heard in the dark; the men were frighten by the sound and began to huddle together; never had any of them heard sounds as those before.

They looked to Coot for protection.

Kapier assured no harm would befall them at all just do as Coot ordered. Dar and Armiee felt no fear.

 As they sat quietly on the branches of Kapier's friends; while the other tall trees were waiting to go to war with Coot.

 The green stone began to shine very bright once more inside O'Dea's pocket; he took the stone out and placed it on the forest floor.

The tall trees were not affected by the light at all; it helped all to see the ugliness of the forest; Dar couldn't believe what she was looking at!

The trees didn't have leaves on them at all or bark; they looked old and dry rotten.

It brought tears to Kapier's eyes including his friends; because they remembered long ago how beautiful the trees were.

The light from the stone continued to shine brightly; Coot and the others waited patiently For Wog.

Some of the men that was seated on the forest floor began to slump over dead.

Coot knew the reason why!

Wog had released a mist of slime gas in the air; Coot ordered them to climb up the trees; the trees helped them to reach higher grounds to escape the mist of gas; O'Dea remained on the branch of Kapier.

Coot was alone on the forest floor.

Wog's slime gas had no effect on him at all.

He had been breathing the gas for over hundred years.

Out of the darkness came Wog.

The hundreds of men that were in the trees began to get frighten once more.

Coot asked them.

If all of you come here to destroy me.

How the Shit!

You cowards were going to do it?

Now I see how this slime ball made slaves of some of you.

Never as a man were I frighten of anything.

Something I inherited from my Father; and to add to his memory.

I will slay this evil slime ball and set you cowards free once and for all.

Coot saw Wog's ghastly creatures trying to climb the tall trees to get the humans; especially the two women.

The trees were swatting them if they were flies; ghastly creatures were flying in the air hitting against the old battered trees.

Wog slimed close to Coot.

I didn't come here to kill you he said to Coot.

I only was pretending.

Why would I kill you?

WAIT!

You are human again!

Yes!

Coot said to it.

Kill it now!

Yelled Kapier.

Coot placed an arrow upon its bow once more and let it flow.

Hitting Wog in his large eye!

A big burst of slime exploded from it!

Splashing on the old dry rotten trees!

The trees began to grow beautiful greenery on them; Wog's ghastly remaining creatures return once again into men.

 Coot walked through the slime; after his arrow returned to him and was placed with the others.

 Kapier asked his friends to stand apart; when they notice the Sun shining brightly in a beautiful blue sky.

Sunlight lit up the forest.

The stone immeadally stop shining its light.

Coot went to Wog's slimy dead body; with a large stick in his hands; he touched it and what happen next was unreal.

A man emerged from Wog's remains.

It was Dar's Father!

Kapier asked his river friends.

Let loose your waters on the forest floor; wash all the evil slime away once and for all; the men climbed down the trees and helped rid the forest floor of Wog and his dead ghastly creatures.

Dar asked the tree to put her down; she ran to her Father and embraced him tightly; tears of joy were running down her cheeks; he held his daughter close.

Father!

You think my brother is still alive too?

My daughter.

I have no memory of what happen to him; I have no memory of me; living inside of that slimy creature; All I can say is; I'm happy I'm no longer inside of it; and happy to see you once again.

Your Brother might be at his slimy castle with the others Coot said to them; Dar looked at her father and noticed he hadn't aged at all.

Tell me Father, do you have any memory at all what happen to you, my brother and the others?

Some of the men were still in awe!

Seeing Coot's arrow return to him after killing Wog's slimy-ass. (Reader one more time, close your eyes and vision, slime from a Trillion snails)

Coot began to look for his hunters.

No way they are still alive; only I was granted longevity of life; my hunters are dead and I am to blame; when I was transformed; I turned them into ghastly creatures of my own.

O'Dea embraced his wife very tightly; begging her to forgive him.

He turned and walked up to Coot and said.

Great hunter.

Can we please see our daughter?

The others were asking can they keep the jewels; they had packed to the tilt in their bags.

Yes!

All of you can keep your jewels.

Never will the people of your lands hunger again; the rivers have washed the other jewels away forever; go back to your lands and live happy and rich for a long time.

Remember!

Do not to take back hate, envy and cruelty; be good to each other until the end of all times.

Coot turned to O'Dea and his wife and asked them.

Follow me.

When they made it to his woods; they were amazed at what they were looking at.

A mighty kingdom made of pure gold and diamonds. He brought them to a large diamond and golden door. The door was un-locked with a diamond key.

When the door was open.

In the grand room stood their beautiful daughter. They wanted to run and embrace her.

Coot gently asked.

Wait!

He went to her first and removed the silk band from her eyes.

She also had a golden crown with diamonds on top of her head; after the silk band was removed she looked Coot in the face and asked.

Are you my keeper?

Yes Coot answered.

I forgive you my keeper she said to him, with tears in her beautiful hazel eyes.

Coot said to her very softly.

Now I can say out loud your name; I only said with my heart for many years.

Jewel.

Coot pointed to her parents and said.

They have been waiting a very long time to hold you close, my precious Jewel.

Please tell me my keeper.

Who are they?

Then tell me when you changed.

I never seen you look as this before; in my memories you were an animal of some sort; please explain that to me; I never seen creatures like them before. I still don't know what I look like.

I saw you several times.

Knowing I was taking a risk in doing so; but now you stands before me looking differently.

Where is my real keeper?

Where are the others that took care of me?

Coot took her by the hand; he asked her parents to remain still.

I am going to take a walk with Jewel and explain to her what has taken place he said to them.

Jewel walked with Coot around his large estate; he began talking with her about long ago; some she understood and majority she did not have a clue.

So the creatures in the yard are the natural keepers of me?

I belong to them and not you?

The servants at Coot's mansion were no longer ghastly looking at all.

They too were now men!

Try to understand more clearly Jewel, Coot asked her. .

The harrow is over.

Wog is no longer or his others; he's the one that helped in transforming me into the monster you remember.

I'm too is free!

We are humans!

Now!

Let's go back to your Mother and Father; so you can be embraced by them; they waited a very long time for this day.

As they were walking back Coot notice several people in his front yard; Dar her father, O'Dea and his wife; several of the men that had come to the dark forest in destroying him.

One of his servants call out to him.

What about the people that has gathered here Master Coot!

Do we slay them all?

No!

Let them be!

We are all free now!

The dark forest is no longer dark; Wog and some of his is no longer here.

Look at your selves!

Remove the covering from all mirrors!

This is the day to rejoice; we are human's again not monsters of Wog anymore.

Let's celebrate!

Jewel ran to her parents!

They embraced her as tears flowed from their eyes; Dar was very happy for them; but she still longed to see her brother's face.

What a celebration!

Coot stood and said!

Look!

Every-one saw a little very dirty toad-man entering the yard; Coot know of it.

Come my little one!

Come!

The little one-eye toad-man refuse to take another step toward any of them . He only stood blinking his one eye.

Dar felt pity and went to him; he looked so pitiful and filthy dirty with traces of slime on him.

Dar bent over with tears of sadness in her eyes; she said to him.

Do not be afraid little one.

No harm is to come to you here; as she was speaking a single tear dropped in his one eye.

Low and behold standing tall!.

Dar's brother.

Shouting of joy was heard through-out the kingdom, even back in the forest; Kapier and his friends were shouting out loud too; even more shouting was heard.

Wog's slimy castle has been washed away for-ever; the little one eye toad man made a very narrow escape; to the safety of Coot's golden castle just in time.

Dar and her father held him close for longest time; happy seeing him well and alive.

How did all this happen Father?

Last I remember we were walking in the dark forest and you slipped on slime that was on the forest floor; what happen after that I have no memory at all.

Tell me!

How did I get here?

Who all these people?

Is that our new kingdom and the people of our new land is here to celebrate?

Where's Mother?

My son all your questions will have answers to them.

Not Now!

Dar's Father Name is King Lardar, her brother's name is Prince Aydra and her mother's name is Queen Dexayma.

The celebration at Coot's mansion lasted days on end; back in the forest Kapier and his friends had things under control.

The other trees in the forest were no longer dry rotten anymore; they were tall and beautiful again; Kapier and his friends return back to the entrance of the forest.

No longer would they need to warn anyone about Coot or the evil thing that dwelled there any-more.

Now they can be only trees.

No magical enchantment would they have.

Kapier and the others return to their original spot ; there they would remain until the end of all times.

Never to speak again.

Meanwhile back at Coot's castle the celebration was still going on; O'Dea's wife continue to hug and kiss her daughter's face; others were telling tall tales when each of them venture in the dark forest long ago.

Dar and her reunited ones were making plans returning to her land to surprise her Mother and the people.

King Lardar spoke out loud!

Great hunter!

With your permission!

I would love to live in your new forest, me and my people;

See!

We live in a land where the Sun goes away for one year; the forest would be perfect for my people and me.

Yes Father Dar said.

It would be the perfect place; no longer would our people hunger; the children would love living in the forest and think how happy our old would be also.

Yes mighty king!

You and your people are welcome to live there!

Thank you mighty hunter!

We shall leave at once, I will return with our young and our old; live out our lives in peace and harmony.

Coot turned his attention to Jewel's parents.

Believe me when I tell you, your daughter was not harmed by me at all; I only pretend to harm her to keep her safe from that slime-ball I slayed and his others.

The first time she looked at me with her beautiful eyes and smiled.

I knew then!

I would never bring her harm or let anything harm her. I kept her safe from Wog and his ghastly creatures.

No way!

I would had let her live in slime the rest of her life, being filthy, hungry, beaten and worked to almost dead.

To think her food would been a slimy mess to eat every day.

No!

I was not about to let that happen; even if it caused me my miserable life.

And!

Please believe me when I say

I lived in misery.

Until!

You O'Dea!

Venture into my woods.

When you brought her to me O'Dea; my days were no longer.

Long as Shit!

I had someone to brighten my days.

I watched her grow.

Now she's the beauty that has capture my heart for-ever.

I remember you great hunter Jewel spoke and said.

I remember what you looked like before and I was never afraid.

Why would I be? She snickered.

When all around me looked the same.

The way all of you look now is what's confusing.

Let us forget about long ago Coot said.

Today is what's important!

No more will you live in darkness, and you will forever see my face.

Come!

Let us continue celebrating.

King Lardar was preparing to leave, when he turned to Coot and asked.

Tell me great hunter where do you go from here? Are you going to venture back to your home again?

I have no memory of finding my home anymore Great King. I have lived in these woods over a hundred years.

This is my home now.

This forest is all I know; the sun shines here now the forest is beautiful again, flowers are blooming; I saw a beautiful blue bird nesting in its nest.

No!

I have no desire to venture to a place that's unknown to me now.

He turned to Jewel.

Be my bride and live with me here in my woods; you would want for nothing long as you live, especially me.

Jewel looked at her Father and Mother.

Would the two of you be angry at me; if I say I wants to remain with him in his woods?

No Daughter!

They both said at the same time.

Remember!

You was given to him long ago.

Coot was happy from what he just heard from her parents; they stayed with them a while longer.

Then it was time for them to leave.

The others had been left, with their riches of course; some had no idea in finding their way back to their lands.

So.

The first lands some went to; is where they stayed and live rich ever after; not remembering anything about the dark forest at all, especially re-turning to get more jewels.

(Reader! Now you know! Ain't no way! I was going to let they greedy asses return to get more jewels…lmao)

O'Dea asked Coot.

So tell me great hunter!

Will you for-ever be called Coot?

Sadly thinking about his long gone parents; and the name that was given to him at birth Swoot; the name he love to be called by women, Coot; a name that also brought hardship on him too.

No O'Dea!

I no longer will be called Coot; my name that will be for-ever called.

Is Bubba!

Laughing out loud O'Dea said.

Bubba you shall be called then.

After they left for their home; O'Dea had a talk with his wife.

Listen to me Armiee!

Before leaving Bubba's woods

I had a talk with him concerning the green stone; he told me the stone has power of everlasting life.

Only to ones that deserve it.

No one we know deserve to live forever.

Including us.

He did say we will live a very long time never growing old.

We can't return to our land looking this young; many of the people have died off, and for us to return now!

Would cause problems!

I told Bubba the land we will be living on; I also told him we wouldn't be wealthy at all.

Just regular people!

As a matter of fact!

I have no memory.

When we want to visit our daughter again; I don't know the direction to lead us back at all.

DO YOU?

No O'Dea I don't!

Has it accrued to you at all?

You been tricked by that monster again; look behind us ; tell me what you see?

Looking behind them was no path at all; only a path that led them forward; O'Dea remembered who's name now is Bubba, told him long ago.

Your daughter is to live with me forever.

His wife walked closer to him and slapped him hard across his face drawing blood from his nose; same as she done years ago.

O'Dea had to think hard about it ; he knew they were never to see their daughter again after all; they walked in silence a long time; when his wife began to speak with him.

Tell me dumb-ass man!

Where are we to live? Since we can't return to our home. What about your riches that are there? This path is leading us to a land; where no one knows how wealthy you are.

We only have the few jewels that were taken from the dark forest; how long you think these jewels would last us?

O'Dea pointed and said, I see people ahead, do not talk to anyone; about what happen in the dark forest; do not mention to anyone about Coot.

As they walked closer to the people; some were looking at them strangely; O'Dea heard some whispering to each other saying.

Wonder where those old people come from? A man come up to them and asked.

Old timers are you all lost?

Do you have family in this land? Are you hungry? Can I find you a place to rest your weary bodies?

O'Dea couldn't understand why the man was calling them old; until he saw their images on a store glass window; they did look very old and haggard; Both of them had hair of gray, wrinkles all over their faces and a hump in each back.

The young man was being concerned about the two very old people; he asked them to follow him to a place where they could rest and eat.

Then he would take them to a place where they would sleep for the night; until he could figure out how to help them further; O'Dea's wife whispered to him.

How we aged this way?

That monster allowed us to walk down a path knowing it was the path; that would help us to become our true age; you let that monster really trick your dumb ass this time.

The young man had another man with him; he asked them to follow him; he took them to a very large house with many rooms; people were being very nice to them.

A woman asked O'Dea's wife.

Grand-mother can I help you with anything? You need not to be afraid.

The people of the land take very good care of the old. Come grand-mother eat and rest yourself.

The young man was aiding to O'Dea as well; O'Dea pulled out a golden coin from his pocket; to his amazement; the young man told him. No grand-father there is no need of payment from you at all; the two of you living this long is all the payment that is required.

This is the land for the dying of the old.

O'Dea hung his head again.

He had to accept the fact they is never to see their daughter again. Both of them let the young cater to their every need, they no longer had to do anything but grow older and die.

Final Chapter

Years had passed away.

Bubba and Jewel had children of their own, identical twin sons and one beautiful daughter, children that had no grand-parents to spoil them only their parents.

Bubba twin boys were a hand full, they cared nothing for bow and arrows. They only cared for guns and horses.

Their mother didn't care for the noise that come from them at all. She let their father deal with them in that category.

One bright sunny day Bubba an Jewel had a visitor. The person had very sad news to tell them, he told them the dying of Jewel's parents. Bubba was watching how his wife was reacting to the news; there has to be a reason why she was acting that way.

Well he found out why!

She said to him.

When my parents left our woods, I knew I would never see them again, but I could see them at times with this; she open her hand in it laid the green stone.

How long you had that stone Bubba asked?

I want you to listen to me my darling husband and please do not interrupt me; he didn't interrupt her, but her sons did, from shooting their guns like crazy at birds flying by.

BOYS!

PUT YOUR GUNS AWAY!

NOW!

She screamed. Your father and I is trying to have a serious conversation; she asked her nanny to take them in the woods, to continue shooting at birds.

Her attention went back to her husband.

As I was saying.

This stone been in my keep for several years, I was never to tell you about it, if I had mention it to you, I would never been able to see my mother and father at times.

NO!

I couldn't speak to them, only see their faces; I saw how old they had become, I ask the stone where were they, and was told it was for-bidden for it to say.

I ask the stone did it have power to give them everlasting life,

 I was told no.

The stone told me yesterday about them dying; I asked the stone once more, to grant them everlasting life. The stone said to me, today is the last time I will speak to you, after this talk throw me away.

You will not hear anything from me again, I too must die, and same as you and Coot (not Bubba) will do one day. Never will you two live to see your kids die.

Now throw me away!

Bubba asked his wife are you finish talking.

He said listen to me my precious Jewel.

Dying is something we all must do; your parents lived a very long time; so have you and I.

Let's rejoice in their passing and continue being happy and alive together with our children; let dying be the last thing we think about.

OK?

Armiee went and laid in her husband's chest and spoke softly saying.

Yes!

I will try not to think of dying again; I have been with you all my life, I know no other as I know you, not even my children.

The servants are bothered with them more than me; it don't mean I don't love them, I only knows how to be with you.

Bubba held her close as she wept; because he know she's right about it all. He closed his eyes and let his mind take him back to all the years gone by.

Never once he let his mind take him to the time, when he was a monster name Coot, thinking about the hundreds of years, he lived in the dark forest with Wog and the other ghastly creatures; now he's human again with wife and children, even though he changed his name to Bubba; Coot is really the name he wants to be for-ever called.

Thinking about the years gone by when he was the greatest hunter in all the lands; his Father's Kingdom was greatest of all too; how he was loved by majority of the women of the lands; If only he could turn back the hand of time; holding his wife Jewel as she weeps from the dying of her parents; never she's to know he's the one that sat them on the path; that would lead them to the dying land for the old; she's never to know him too has a green stone and how often he talks with his friend Kapier; he's the only human that knows Kapier still speaks; Jewel brought him out of his deep thinking by asking him; how long will she mourn the death of her parents?

As long you need to he replied; why mourn for two people you only knowed for a short time?

I am very confused Jewel said to him.

She lifted herself from him and went in search of her children; thinking as she looked for them; today from this forward I'm going to be more involved in their lives; I am their Mother, no longer will I let the servants be the ones to take of their needs more than I.

My husband has enough to deal with; especially when it comes to being the protector of his woods.

Coot looked at his wife as she walked away. He were thinking on paying a visit to his old friend Kapier. Who happens to be a human now, no one is to know he's the one brought news of the dying of Jewel's parents.

Coot (not Bubba) knows it's time to let go of his past; he's in control of a very beautiful and large forest, with good people that dwells in it; His friend Kapier is to know of being human; and remain close to Coot and his family for all times.

The End.

Dedicated To My Baby Sister, Arrilla Kaye-Thompson-Kelly our Mother's(late Mrs. Cynthia Ree Thompson) 18th Child…..Thanks for reading…Jupie…

Made in the USA
Columbia, SC
24 February 2024